THE BRAD FORREST ADVENTURE SERIES

BRAD FORREST'S
HALIFAX ADVENTURE

BRAD FORREST

Bradley Raymond Forrest was born in Ottawa but he grew up in Toronto where his father's newspaper empire has its headquarters. Mr. Forrest owns a farm in Quebec and a Montreal house, so during the holidays Brad learned to speak French fluently.

He is taking Political Science at the University of Toronto and he plays hockey, golf and football; he is keen on skiing and small-car racing and, as a flier, he has his multi-engine ticket. Hunting and skeet shooting have made him a fair shot and mountain climbing, skin diving and riding have kept him very fit. Although Mr. Forrest is very wealthy, he believes that his son should earn his holidays, so Brad has done all sorts of jobs in the newspaper business when not engaged in disentangling himself from his many fascinating and sometimes dangerous adventures.

HALIFAX ADVENTURE

Brad Forrest expects to enjoy covering the story of the search for treasure on Oak Island but sudden danger threatens when Captain Scott of the Royal Canadian Navy reveals to him and to Conn Casey, a young fisherman, that the investigation is being impeded by an unknown gang of crooks who are after something even more valuable than the treasure. To help track down the crooks and their mysterious objective, Brad goes to sea aboard a merchant ship and also an RCN destroyer, and the solution of one mystery clears up another—the fate of a young officer who had been cashiered from the Navy.

Brad Forrest's
HALIFAX
ADVENTURE

BY
HUGH MAITLAND

LONGMANS CANADA LIMITED
TORONTO

© Longmans Canada Limited, 1965

All rights reserved. No part of this book may be reproduced in any form without permission in writing from the publisher, except by a reviewer who may quote brief passages in a review to be printed in a magazine or newspaper.

PRINTED AND BOUND BY
HAZELL WATSON AND VINEY LTD
AYLESBURY, BUCKS, ENGLAND

CONTENTS

1	To Oak Island	9
2	Dwight Davis	16
3	Conn Casey	24
4	Sinking Diver	31
5	The Dig Attacked	38
6	Dynamite	44
7	Surprise Meeting	51
8	New Operators	57
9	17 Hamilton Street	63
10	"Le Grand"	70
11	Into the Ocean	78
12	Ops Room	84
13	Fog	91
14	Missing Ship	98
15	Mysterious Bush	103
16	Underground Fight	111
17	"Esther" Explodes	119
18	Captured	128
19	Away Boarders!	135
20	Grounded	144
21	Davis Captured	151

W. Wheeler

CHAPTER 1

To Oak Island

"Brad! Brad Forrest!"

The office boy in the Forrest Newspaper Syndicate's Montreal office stopped Brad on his way out the door.

"The M. E. wants to see you," called the boy, dashing away on another errand.

Brad turned back into the busy office and walked across the huge newsroom toward George Archer's office.

As the Managing Editor of the Forrest Newspaper Syndicate, Mr. Archer was responsible for assigning his writers to their various jobs.

Brad Forrest, six feet tall, well built and with a blond crew hair cut, was the son of Raymond Forrest, president of the Forrest Newspaper Enterprises. Included in the Forrest group were newspapers, magazines, television stations and syndicate offices spread around the world.

Brad was a second year Political Science student at the University of Toronto and was spending the summer working for the syndicate side of his father's business. The fact that his father owned the business made no difference to the way he'd been assigned to stories during the summer. He'd covered the drab and the interesting features that are an everyday part of a feature writer's life and the boy hadn't complained.

He'd just finished a feature on Montreal's old hotels and when he knocked on George Archer's door he hoped his next assignment would be more interesting.

"You did a good job on that hotel piece, Brad," snapped Archer. "I know it was a lousy thing to work on and I hope this one will be better."

Brad smiled but he only said, "Thank you, sir," though he wondered what was coming next. When he remembered some of the adventures he'd had, he hoped it wouldn't turn out to be too exciting.

Four hours later the boy was on a TCA Vanguard bound for Halifax!

After getting his assignment he'd had a quick look at the office files for some background information on the story, packed and rushed out to Montreal's International Airport just in time to board his flight.

When he settled back in his seat, it was his first chance to think about the story he was to cover.

To Oak Island

"I want you to go to Halifax," George Archer had said, "and get me a series of features on the people working on the Oak Island treasure.

"A Captain Fred Scott, a wartime friend of your father's, has gotten leave of absence from the Navy, some financial backing from some of his Halifax friends, and has been working away on the Oak Island treasure since July 1st—about six weeks ago.

"Have a look at the files for some background dope on the Oak Island treasure and when you get down there let's have about ten pieces spread out over three weeks."

"*Yes, sir!*" said Brad, brightly. This *did* sound more interesting than the Montreal hotel story.

Archer turned back to the papers on his desk and Brad knew there would be no more information necessary.

The boy turned to leave the office when Archer called him back.

"When you're down there, nose around and see if you can get any more dope on Peter Grey. The official version of why he was kicked out of the Navy has never satisfied me. Also, there was a wire story about that ship from Istanbul that was damaged in a storm a couple of days ago. Apparently it's being repaired but the ship are doing the repairs themselves. They won't let anybody else on board."

When the aircraft levelled off for the flight east,

Brad Forrest pulled out the notes he'd made on the Oak Island treasure and began to refresh his memory.

Oak Island was in Mahone Bay, not too far down the coast from Halifax and for nearly 200 years one group after another had been searching for a treasure presumed to have been buried there by Captain Kidd.

Brad's information wasn't as complete as he would have liked it to be, but he knew it was fairly firmly established that there was treasure on the island.

Nobody really knew whether it had belonged to Captain Kidd but in 1849 one of the diggers, using a primitive drill, had brought up a piece of golden chain and a jewel.

Though both were eventually lost, this encouraged the diggers, but once again the ingenious system of tide traps had foiled them as it had done every other group that had tried to dig for the Oak Island treasure.

Brad didn't know what the "tide traps" were but he was sure he'd find out when he got to Oak Island.

There was plenty of information on Lieutenant Peter Grey.

His dishonourable release from the Canadian Navy had been a page one story in all of the North

American newspapers and many overseas, for weeks.

Accused of handing official secrets to a foreign power, Lieutenant Grey had been court-martialled and then discharged. The papers had carried details of his naval career but their information about the trial was sketchy.

The name of the person or country to whom he'd passed the secrets was never released and Grey hadn't been sent to jail.

He'd just disappeared when he'd been discharged.

By the time the Vanguard had slipped into a smooth landing at Halifax, and Brad had taxied the twenty odd miles from the airport to the city, it was nearly midnight and too late to get out to Oak Island.

The boy checked into the Nova Scotian Hotel and went to bed. He wanted an early start in the morning and there was nothing he could do that night to get more information on his story.

Next morning Brad discovered there were buses from Halifax to Chester, where he could hire a boat to take him to Oak Island, but there wasn't one until nearly noon.

Walking up through the narrow, sleezy streets toward Barrington Street, Brad was charmed with the ancient air about Halifax. In spite of the modern harbour facilities and the good hotels, the city seemed to be as settled and as quiet as a small village.

His ideas about Halifax changed somewhat when the bus swept him out past the modern Camp Hill hospital, past Armdale and then abruptly into the country.

The change from city to country happened so fast he could hardly believe it. One minute they were sweeping up past the "Arm" and the next the bus was speeding past farms that looked deserted and broken down.

But Chester looked exactly like the small town Brad imagined it was. The boy thought the town seemed to be acknowledging the twentieth century reluctantly, as though it resented the retired Naval officers who made up the majority of its population.

There wasn't a taxi to take him down to the jetties so, carrying his Gladstone bag, Brad Forrest walked toward Mahone Bay and toward the most exciting adventure he'd ever had.

The jetties looked as though they would be liable to fall down at any moment but the wooden piles were weatherworn and probably had been there for a hundred years.

At the end of one of the fishing jetties, at a part of Chester known as The Peninsula, Brad joined an old man who was staring out over the sunlit waters of the bay, as though counting the hundreds of islands.

"Can I rent a boat to take me out to Oak Island?"

Slowly the old man turned and stared at Brad.

"Oak Island, bye?" he said, slowly taking the pipe from his mouth. "There's nothing but death and bad luck out there!"

CHAPTER 2

Dwight Davis

"Nonsense!"

The sharp, clipped voice came from behind Brad and the boy swung around.

The man who'd spoken was heavy set, without being fat and had the bluest and coldest eyes Brad had ever seen. He was showing his teeth in a grin that didn't reach his eyes and extending his hand to the boy. Brad noticed the hand was tanned and on the little finger the man wore a peculiar signet ring.

"I'm Dwight Davis," he said. "My yacht, 'Esther', is at anchor out near Oak Island and I'd be glad to take you out there."

Brad took the stranger's hand and when he introduced himself, he noticed the man's yachting costume.

"I'll be glad to give you a ride out to Oak Island," Davis went on. "No matter what this old timer says, there's lots of activity out there."

When Brad and Davis left the jetty in the yachtsman's inboard cruiser, the boy looked back to see the old man leaning against one of the fish houses shaking his head in sorrow.

"First time you've been down here, son?" Davis asked, cheerily.

"Yes, it is," said Brad with a smile. Then he told the older man about the features he would be writing on the Oak Island treasure.

Mahone Bay was 20 miles long and 12 miles wide and Brad was to find out there were 365 islands scattered throughout it. Aside from the odd summer cabin, most of them were uninhabited but the most activity was taking place on Oak Island.

"For over 150 years, people have been trying to solve the mystery of the Oak Island treasure," Davis was saying, while he steered his boat across the sunlit bay. "I wouldn't be surprised if Captain Scott manages to be the one to finally find it."

"Has he gotten very far down?" Brad asked.

"I don't think so. He's digging in the exact spot where most of the other treasure hunters have—right under the oak tree—but so far I don't think he's discovered much."

From Chester out to Oak Island is a couple of miles and as the boat bounced along the chop, Davis identified some of the islands for Brad.

"That's Gooseberry Island and Little Gooseberry Island," he said pointing, "and over there's Frog Island and Big Fish Island."

"None of them have oak trees," Brad observed.

Davis laughed. "I know they don't. That's one of the mysteries. There are very few oak trees north of Virginia, except on Oak Island. There's nothing else there aside from some native shrubs."

There were really two parts to Oak Island, one large and one small and they were nearly separated by a deep indentation with a power line running across it.

Davis turned his cruiser under the power line and brought it to a stop near a huge rock that jutted out from a gravel beach.

"That's the rock that had the iron securing ring buried in it," Davis explained. "It was the discovery of this ring in 1795 that started the searches for the Oak Island treasure."

Beyond the rock, Brad could see a thick stand of oak trees and underneath one, near the southern promontory of the island, there were several men working. When the cruiser's engine stopped, Brad could hear the thump, thump of a motor ashore that was driving a pump.

"Thanks for the lift," Brad called, when he wrestled his bag and portable typewriter ashore.

"I'll be seeing you again," Davis replied, with

a wave of his hand, "you and Captain Scott must come out to 'Esther' for dinner."

When Dwight Davis backed his boat away from the shore, Brad turned inland. Davis was certainly pleasant enough but Brad couldn't get over a feeling of dislike he had for the man.

"Maybe it's his eyes," Brad thought. "They never seem to be anything else but cold."

It didn't take the boy long to make his way past the workers under the oak tree and find the man in charge of the party.

"So," said Captain Scott, heartily, "you're Ray Forrest's boy."

Brad liked Captain Scott immediately. The Naval officer was tall and thin with a face tanned almost mahogany after years spent on the world's oceans. He showed Brad the layout of the camp and the tent he would be using. All of the tents in the camp were built on wooden platforms and it looked as though the camp was here to stay.

When the boy tossed his bag and typewriter into the tent, Captain Scott said, "Let's have a look around."

With the tall Naval officer, who was dressed in khaki work clothes, Brad walked through the stand of oak trees and the undergrowth toward the dig.

"People have been calling it 'the money pit' for years," said Captain Scott, "and all the old timers in Chester are laughing at me for spending all this money and time trying to solve the mystery of the treasure."

"Have you found anything?" Brad asked, eagerly.

Captain Scott laughed. "That's why the people in Chester are laughing," he said. "All we've found is more evidence that there is some kind of a treasure, or at least some oak chests buried under the tree. The chests were originally discovered in 1803."

The excavation Brad saw was now about fifteen feet deep and about twenty feet wide. Some of the men working in the hole were digging and the rest were shoring up the walls as they went further and further into the earth.

Over the hole was a huge wooden frame-work supporting a drill that disappeared in the hole and running beside the drill was a canvas hose that jumped back and forth with each thump of the pump.

"We're trying to get as much water out as we can before we get too far down," Captain Scott explained. "It's been the flooding of the excavation that's stopped all the diggers in the past."

"What happens?" asked the boy.

Captain Scott wiped the sweat off his forehead before he replied. "I wish I knew exactly. We do know there are at least two channels dug from somewhere inside the pit leading toward the shore. These channels seem to work with the tide and even the most modern equipment hadn't managed to keep the water out.

"Every night when the men stop working, we're careful to get the horizontal shores tight in place so if there is any flooding, the sides of the hole won't cave in. We've got the best pumps money can buy and hope to be able to clear the water out in a hurry."

For an hour, Brad and the Captain watched the men working. The going was slow but there wasn't any sign of the flooding that seemed to worry Captain Scott.

Later in the afternoon, Brad and the Captain left the dig and walked down to the south-eastern tip of the island on their way to the camp.

"There's Davis' yacht," said Captain Scott. "It's anchored off Sam Island, a funny place to anchor I've thought."

"What do you mean, sir?" Brad asked.

Captain Scott seemed to want to get away from the subject. "I don't know, Brad. Davis is supposed to be on a vacation but he doesn't do anything but run back and forth into Chester in that cruiser."

"Let's walk around to the other side of the island," said Brad.

"Not right now," said the Captain, tersely. "There's nothing over there to see but the power line running over to Grandall Point on the mainland. I've got some notes to work on and I suppose you should be filing your first story."

Brad was surprised at the way the affable Captain was keeping him away from the south-east side of the island but he dismissed the thought from his mind.

The boy did a background feature on the Oak Island treasure, using the information he'd gotten from Captain Scott and the files in Montreal. Then, after supper, he took one of the small boats with an outboard motor and went into Chester to file his story.

Rather than use the busy Government Wharf, Brad tied his boat at the fish wharf he'd used in the morning.

As he walked back down the jetty toward the bollard he'd used, his rubber soled shoes made no sound on the wooden planks. Near the end he paused, when he heard voices coming from around the corner of the fish shed.

It was Dwight Davis' voice!

"Don't worry," the yachtsman was saying, "we'll get them away from there soon and they won't find anything anyway." The man's voice was cracking with anger.

Brad stepped back hurriedly, he didn't want to be caught eavesdropping.

As he retreated, he half turned, just in time to catch a glimpse of his attacker.

In the dim light, his eye caught something descending on his head.

Lights exploded!

He half lost consciousness and then felt the waters of Chester harbour close over his head.

CHAPTER 3

Conn Casey

THE SHOCK of the ever-cold waters of Chester Harbour closing over the boy's head brought him partly back to his senses. He struggled toward the surface but once again the mist closed over his brain and he felt himself slipping below.

But Brad Forrest wouldn't give up that easily. Even though half conscious, he still struggled, once again, into the fading daylight and this time he managed to wave his hands.

As his face dropped below the water level for the third time, he thought he heard somebody shout and saw a form leaping from the jetty to his rescue.

The boy felt a strong hand grip the collar of his windbreaker and just as he swallowed another mouthful of water, he was hauled to the surface.

Brad felt himself coughing and spluttering as his lungs rejected the dirty salt water. He sucked in great mouthfuls of fresh air as he lay on the jetty

Conn Casey

and when the fog cleared from his brain he could see Dwight Davis and a strange boy looking down at him. The boy's clothes were dripping wet.

"Are you all right?" Davis asked, anxiously.

Brad staggered to his feet, still coughing and when he looked into Davis' face he was shocked by the concern he could see there. He was also, again, struck by the coldness of the blue eyes.

"What happened?" said the boy, in a strong down-east accent.

Brad coughed again, stalling for time. He was sure he'd been hit on the head because somebody thought he was eavesdropping on Davis' conversation, but would it be wise to let Davis know this? Was the young man with Davis a confederate of his?

Brad made up his mind quickly. "I don't know," he said. "I thought I might have been hit on the head and tossed into the harbour but that couldn't have happened. I must have had a dizzy spell and then hit my head on a piling when I fell."

"Good thing you came along, boy," said Davis, turning his evil eyes on the youth in fisherman's clothes.

"Thanks," said Brad. "I'm Brad Forrest."

"I'm Conn Casey," said the boy.

When Brad shook Conn's hand, he could feel the rough calluses that came from years of handling ropes soaked in salt water.

"I was just comin' 'round the corner of the fish house here," said Conn, "when I heard somebody fall in the water."

"Good thing," said Brad, heartily. He wondered if Davis or the man he'd been talking to would have saved him if Conn hadn't happened to come along.

"Can you get back to Oak Island alone, Brad?" asked Davis. His voice had a note of kindness in it but Brad didn't trust him.

"Oak Island!" said Conn, before Brad could reply. "I was headin' out there to try and find a job. My dory's right under the jetty here."

"I'm OKay, Mr. Davis," said Brad. "I'll take Conn out there with me and even if Captain Scott hasn't got a job for him, I'm sure he can spend the night."

"All right, Brad. I've got an appointment in Chester otherwise I'd insist I take you out to the island myself."

Brad and Conn rode in Captain Scott's boat, towing Conn's dory along behind.

"I won't leave her behind," said Conn. "Never know when I might need her."

Wrapped up in Conn's windbreaker and crouched behind the wind dodger, Brad didn't feel the cold too much. Taking shelter from the wind, he had a chance to talk to the boy who'd hauled him out of the water.

"Did you see anybody else on the jetty when you arrived there?" Brad asked.

"Not a soul," said Conn, cheerfully. "That man Davis was just comin' 'round the other end of the fish house. I didn't wait to see if there was anybody else, I just thought I'd better get you out."

"Thanks again, Conn," said Brad.

"No trouble, Brad. When we get to Oak Island we can change our clothes. I've brought my gear in the duffle bag in the dory."

"Were you that sure you'd get a job?" said Brad, surprised.

"Nah," said Conn, grinning. "If I didn't I'd take the dory out and have a look at my lobster pots and then spend the night on the beach."

"Is working lobster pots all you do?"

Conn grinned again. "Nah! I do anythin' connected with the sea. Deep water fishin', coast fishin' but mostly in the season I get enough lobster to make a livin'."

"Have you always been working near the ocean?"

"Sure! All my life. At least since I was fourteen."

Brad grinned too. Conn was so cheerful, he couldn't help it.

"Where shall we land on Oak Island?" asked Conn, after a few minutes' silence.

"Do you know where the rock is that had the ring in it?" Brad asked.

"Sure I do. I've been on the island hundreds of times."

Brad was amazed at the skill Conn showed in handling the boat, even with the dory dragging behind. He could tell Conn wasn't fooling when he said he'd been around boats all his life.

When the boys came alongside the rock it was pitch dark and just as they bumped, the brilliant beam of a flash cut through the darkness catching the boat in its light.

"That you, Brad?" It was Captain Scott.

"Yes, sir," Brad replied.

"I was getting worried about you," the Naval officer called through the darkness. "I thought you might have trouble finding your way back here in the dark."

"That was easy," called Brad, when he climbed out on the shore.

Quickly the boy explained what had happened to him and how Conn had hauled him out of the water.

"Sure Conn can have a job," said Scott, "we need another man to run a supply boat. We haven't got a tent for him to sleep in tonight but he can come back in the morning."

"There's plenty of room in my tent," said Brad. "Conn can share it."

"OKay. When you've changed your clothes and get settled down I'd like to talk to you for a minute."

Conn carried his gear up to the tent and made himself right at home. While Brad changed his clothes, the Nova Scotian boy thanked him for using his influence with Captain Scott.

"We'll go out to the pots one day," he said. "You might be interested in seein' how we take the lobsters."

"I sure will," said Brad, eagerly.

When Brad Forrest strode off through the darkness to Captain Scott's tent he couldn't help thinking how much he liked Conn, at first sight. He also thought about how little he liked Dwight Davis.

It was Davis Captain Scott wanted to talk about.

"Tell me, in detail, exactly what happened on the jetty," he ordered Brad, sternly.

The boy thought for a minute and then described the incident completely.

"There's no chance that you *did* fall in?"

"Not a chance, sir," Brad said, solemnly.

"Humm!" was all the other replied.

"Who is Dwight Davis, anyway?" Brad asked.

Captain Scott was silent for a long time before he answered.

"I wish I knew for sure," he said. "He told me he'd come up here from somewhere down in the States for a vacation but ever since he arrived there have been things happening to hold us up at the dig."

"What kind of things?"

"Oh, all kinds," said Scott vaguely. "Once his yacht swamped a supply boat, then there was a power supply-line cut and another time somebody put sand in the pump bearings."

"Can't you prove it was Davis?"

"No we can't. I've wondered if he was interested in digging for the treasure himself and just waiting for us to quit."

Brad was full of questions but Capain Scott got up from his camp stool as though he expected the boy to leave.

"We'd better keep our eyes open, Brad," he said. "Maybe we'll be able to prove something."

When Brad crawled into his sleeping bag, Conn was already asleep. The boy's mind was racing with thoughts of the treasure and the things that had happened since he'd left Montreal.

But none of them kept him from sleeping. He dropped off immediately and when Conn shook him roughly awake, Brad thought he'd just been asleep for a moment.

The excited tone of Conn's voice and the sunlight coming through the tent flap drove this thought from his mind.

"Common, Brad!" cried Conn. "The dig's caved in!"

CHAPTER 4

Sinking Diver

IT TOOK just a second for Brad to absorb the information, then he leaped to his feet reaching for his clothes.

"Call Captain Scott!" he snapped.

Conn dashed out on the errand and Brad finished dressing. When the boy bolted out of his tent and into the morning sunlight, Scott and Conn were leaving for the site of the dig.

Already the information had spread and a half dozen of the sleepy-looking workmen were standing, staring down into the hole. Through the pile of mud and timbers the lead from the pump was still in place and Brad could hear its thump.

"Glad it's still operating," he thought.

"Too bad, sir," said one of the workmen when Brad, Conn and the Captain arrived.

Scott just stared down into the hole.

"I wonder if it was an accident?" he murmured softly.

Brad wondered too and the boy was determined to find out. Leaping down into the hole, he brushed some of the mud away from the edge of the broken timbers.

His examination gave him the information he wanted.

"It was no accident, sir," he called up to the Captain.

The tall Naval officer didn't reply. He jumped down into the hole to see the piece of timber Brad was holding up.

"Look, sir!" the boy snapped, pointing to the sawn edge of one of the horizontal shores.

Scott ran his hand over the smooth portion that had nearly been sawn through.

"You're right, Brad, something else to delay us."

Together the two climbed to the top of the hole and the Captain started to give some swift orders. The men were told to have their breakfast and get started again.

"This won't happen again," said the Captain finally. "From now on we'll have a guard at this spot twenty-four hours a day."

With that the Captain turned away from the money pit and started back toward the camp.

"Just a minute," called one of the workmen. The

Sinking Diver 33

man's voice was surly and when he stepped out of the group Brad thought he looked familiar.

"If we're goin' to have to stand sentry," the man snarled, "I hope we're goin' to get paid for it."

Captain Scott's tall frame tightened and then gradually relaxed while he studied the man's face. "Arrangements will be made, Jenkins," he said slowly.

For a long second Jenkins stared at Captain Scott and then dropped his eyes.

"I hope so," he said in the same surly tone as he stepped back into the group.

As Brad, Captain Scott and Conn headed back for the camp, Brad wondered if he'd seen Jenkins someplace before.

"That man's been grumbling ever since I hired him," muttered the Captain.

Brad forgot about it when Conn spoke up. "What do you think happened, sir?" he asked.

"I don't know, Conn, but it's just another example of somebody trying to stop us from digging here."

Captain Scott was more determined than ever to keep going. After breakfast he gave Conn his orders for the day. The boy was to check over the supplies and then take a boat into Chester for anything he thought they might need.

"You can help him, Brad," finished the Captain, "or just wander around and gather material for your stories."

"OKay, sir, I think I'll do a little of both."

Brad and Conn worked together in the supply tent for the rest of the morning.

Listening to Conn talk about his years at sea and working the lobster pots, he knew he would have enough information right there to write a personality story about Conn himself.

"How far out in the bay are your traps?" Brad asked, when they'd finished making up the list of supplies they'd need.

"Just around and about, Brad. There's no set place. I can smell lobsters and I move the traps where the lobsters are."

"How do you know which are yours?"

"That's easy. I've got a little flag on the top of each buoy that tells me. Lobster poachin' is a serious crime in the Maritimes, except for the fish."

"The fish! What fish?"

"Black fish. They're great big things like small whales that come in every year and swim through the lines that hold the pot to the buoy. They're so heavy they break the lines and then the pot is gone for good."

"Do you ever see them?" Brad asked.

"Sure we do and so will you too when we go out to look at the pots. They're big all right," laughed Conn.

Sinking Diver

Conn and Brad worked together all during the afternoon. They made several trips into Chester and when Brad arrived at the island after the last one he found Dwight Davis standing with Captain Scott staring down at the men who were busy repairing the damage.

"It's a shame, Captain," Davis was saying when Brad joined them. "You deserve a lot of credit for going on in spite of the trouble you've had."

"We're going on all right," said Scott, with his jaw set in a grim line.

Davis laughed heartily and slapped the tall Captain on the back. "Good! I hope you and Brad will come out to 'Esther' for dinner tonight and I'll try and cheer you up."

Davis turned to the boy. "Will you come, Brad?"

Before Brad replied it flashed through his mind that if there was anything phony about Davis this would be a good chance to look around.

"That would be fine," he said, "if Captain Scott can get away."

"Sure I can," said the Captain.

"Fine," said Davis. Then he turned and left for the spot where his cruiser was moored.

It was nearly ten o'clock when Brad and Captain Scott said good night to Davis and started back for Oak Island in the outboard.

Brad's father's yacht "Svaap" was huge and

luxurious but even the boy had been stunned by the amount of equipment packed into "Esther's" ninety foot length.

"That was some yacht!" said Brad when they'd waved good night to their host.

"It sure was. Davis is a good host but did you notice how careful he was to keep us out of that little room behind the wheel house."

"Yes," said Brad, "and did you also notice that he didn't give us more than a glimpse of the engine room."

The Captain didn't reply, he was looking ahead toward the dim lights on Oak Island. Brad was staring astern at the fading lights of "Esther" when suddenly he heard something crack through the darkness.

"What was that?"

Captain Scott cut the power on the outboard and the boat dropped gently up and down in the swell.

"I thought I heard something too," he said.

In silence the two listened for a minute.

"Sounded like a shot to me," Brad murmured finally.

"Me too!" snapped his friend. Then he cranked the outboard into life. "Let's go back and see."

Scott swung the boat in a tight turn and then steadied its bow straight for "Esther".

Sinking Diver

The sea was on the port bow now and the tiny outboard slapped hard into the waves.

For a few minutes they rushed ahead and then in the darkness Brad saw something black and shiny rising from the water ahead of them.

"Look!" the boy shouted.

Captain Scott had seen the thing too. He swung the boat toward the object and cut the power at the same time.

Slowly they closed the black shape in the water and then suddenly Brad could make out what it was.

"It's a diver!" the boy cried.

"He's hurt too!"

As they watched, the figure in the water lifted one hand in a feeble wave and then slowly started to sink beneath the surface.

"He's sinking!" yelled the Captain.

CHAPTER 5

The Dig Attacked

BRAD HAD recognized the danger for the swimmer before Captain Scott's call. When the Naval officer's shout rang through the darkness, the boy was already pulling off his shoes.

Like a flash, he dove over the boat's side and into the darkness of the water. His dive was shallow but when he surfaced he thought he could see the small disturbance in the water ahead where the diver had disappeared.

The dive had taken him half way and just two strokes brought him to the spot.

Brad duck dived. His eyes were open but they might as well have been closed. The blackness below the surface was complete.

With his powerful legs driving him straight down he swung his arms from side to side feeling for the man who would surely drown if the boy didn't reach him.

The Dig Attacked

It never occurred to Brad to wonder if the man was a crook or not. He was just a human being in need of help.

The boy was barely far enough below the surface for the pressure to have begun to affect his ears, when his right hand brushed against something solid.

Twisting to his right both hands came in contact with the man's shoulders and he felt the heavy tanks on his back. This was what he wanted.

Cupping one hand under the diver's chin, Brad grabbed a handful of his suit and then drove his legs powerfully toward the surface.

When the boy and the man he had rescued came into the clear, night air, Captain Scott had manoeuvred the boat until it was sitting directly beside them.

"OKay, Brad," called Scott, "I've got him! You climb into the boat."

Quickly, Brad levered himself over the boat's gunwale and was just in time to help Scott haul the unconscious man over the side. Totally limp, he flopped in the boat's bottom, like a dead fish.

Reaching down, Brad tore the mask from his face and could tell at a glance he was still breathing. But, seeping from the edge of his hairline was a small trickle of blood.

"My gosh!" cried Scott. "It's Peter Grey!"

Almost as though he'd heard the voice, Grey

opened his eyes. When they fixed on Scott, a flash of something like recognition came into them. He smiled once and then passed out again.

"Let's get him ashore!" cried Scott, turning to the motor.

While Brad stripped the skin-diving suit away from Peter Grey and eased the tanks off his back, Scott took charge of the outboard and headed it, at top speed, for Oak Island.

Rather than tie the boat up at the convenient rock near the dig, Captain Scott rammed it full into the gravel beach near the camp. Working together the Naval officer and the boy carried the limp man into the Captain's tent and rubbed him down with all the towels they could find.

The cut on his head had stopped bleeding and Brad noticed it was almost invisible in the discharged Naval officer's thick hair.

In the excitement, Brad hadn't noticed how cold he was but when Grey started to breathe normally, Scott ordered the boy back to his own tent.

"You go and get out of those wet clothes. I'll look after things here."

Brad was glad to get into some dry things but when he'd changed he hurried back to the Captain's tent.

When the boy brushed aside the tent fly, he realized Grey and the Captain had been whispering

The Dig Attacked

to each other. At the interruption, they drew apart.

"How do you feel?" Brad asked.

"Better now," said Grey, in a cultured voice. "Thanks for saving my life."

Scott's lips were tight and when he spoke Brad could tell he was cross about something. "There's nothing else you can do here tonight," he said. "You might as well go to bed."

"But what was he doing out in the middle of the bay and...."

Scott cut Brad off before he could finish. "I don't know and Grey won't tell me. But I'm sure he was up to no good."

"But..." Brad started again.

"There's no story here for your papers," snapped the Captain. "I'll keep Grey here tonight and tomorrow take him to the police authorities ashore."

"The police!" Brad cried.

"Exactly! The Navy has no interest in what a dishonourably discharged officer was doing in the middle of the night but the civilian people might have some questions to ask."

"I was just out for a swim," said Grey.

"I'll bet," said Brad. "What about the cut on your head? What about the shot?"

"That's enough, Brad!" Scott interrupted. "I'll have to ask you to leave now and say nothing about this."

Puzzled, Brad started out of the tent. He hoped

he would find out sooner or later, but he could tell from the tone of Scott's voice it wouldn't be tonight.

Just outside, Brad turned toward his own tent and as he did so he saw a shadow, or the shadow of a man, slink away from the tent wall.

"Hey!" Brad yelled, loud enough for the man to hear.

He took two giant strides and then launched himself in a flying tackle directly toward the snooper. Just as his feet sought for a firm footing he stepped on a branch and lost his balance.

It was just enough to throw him off stride so he hit the man on one side knocking him down but not hard enough to stay.

Brad leaped to his feet as the man was scuttling away and in the dim light he caught the reflection of a knife poised high enough to be driven into his back.

"Watch it!" There was another cry and another shadow launched itself at Brad's attacker.

It was Conn!

The Nova Scotian hit the man with the knife high, but the boy's yell had been enough warning. Turning, the attacker drove his fist into Conn's chest and when he fell to the ground the man fled into the darkness.

"Whew!" Brad breathed, as he helped Conn to his feet. "Thanks, pal!"

The Dig Attacked

"What's going on here?" It was Captain Scott who came running up to the group.

Brad explained and though he couldn't see the man's face clearly, the boy could tell he was worried.

But Captain Scott had no comment aside from telling Brad to be careful. When the boys went off to their tent the Captain called out.

"We'll have to make sure the guard keeps a good watch tonight."

"I start to stand guard at midnight," said Conn. "I'll be careful."

"You'd better," laughed Brad. "This assignment is turning into more than I expected when I left Montreal."

Conn slept for an hour and when he got up to go on watch Brad woke up enough to tell the boy again to be careful.

"Go to sleep, Brad," Conn chuckled. "I'll watch out for the money pit."

Brad just grunted before he dropped off again. He woke several times during the night and then just after four in the morning he woke again.

This time Conn was shaking him carefully and holding his fingers to his lips, for silence.

"What's the matter?" Brad whispered, instantly awake.

"There're three men sneakin' up to the dig," whispered Conn. "Come on!"

CHAPTER 6

Dynamite

"DID YOU call the Captain?" Brad's whisper was urgent as he hurried with his clothes.

"No," Conn hissed. "There are just three men and they're carrying something heavy between them. I thought too many of us might scare them away and I couldn't do much alone."

When the boys reached the clump of trees near the dig, Conn grabbed Brad's elbow and pulled him down to the ground.

Together they lifted their heads and at the side of the excavation under the tree three men were working rapidly with shovels.

They'd nearly finished burying something and while the boys watched, one of them patted the dirt down hard with a shovel while the other two ran into the woods unreeling wire from a coil.

Conn put his lips close to Brad's ear. "What're they doin'?" he asked.

Dynamite   45

"I think I know," Brad replied quietly. "Common!"

With Conn close behind, Brad cut inland through the trees, taking a wide circle around the dig. He worked his way as quietly as possible through the dark toward the spot where the men with the wire had disappeared.

The darkness had started to fade into daylight now and crouching behind some thick bushes Brad and Conn watched from behind as the men worked quickly with some wires beside a peculiar-looking box that sat on the ground beside them.

Suddenly the three men stood up and one of them pulled a handle straight up from the top of the box.

Brad recognized it immediately.

"That's an electric exploder box," said Brad. "They're going to blow up the pit!"

As he spoke, one of the men reached for the box. Without taking time to explain any more to Conn and hoping the boy would follow him Brad leaped to his feet and charged.

Conn was right behind!

Not caring about noise now, they both let out a yell Brad hoped would be heard in the camp.

"Yip! Yip-e-e-e! Charge men!"

As Brad hoped, the sudden noise and the sound of the charging feet yanked the man's attention

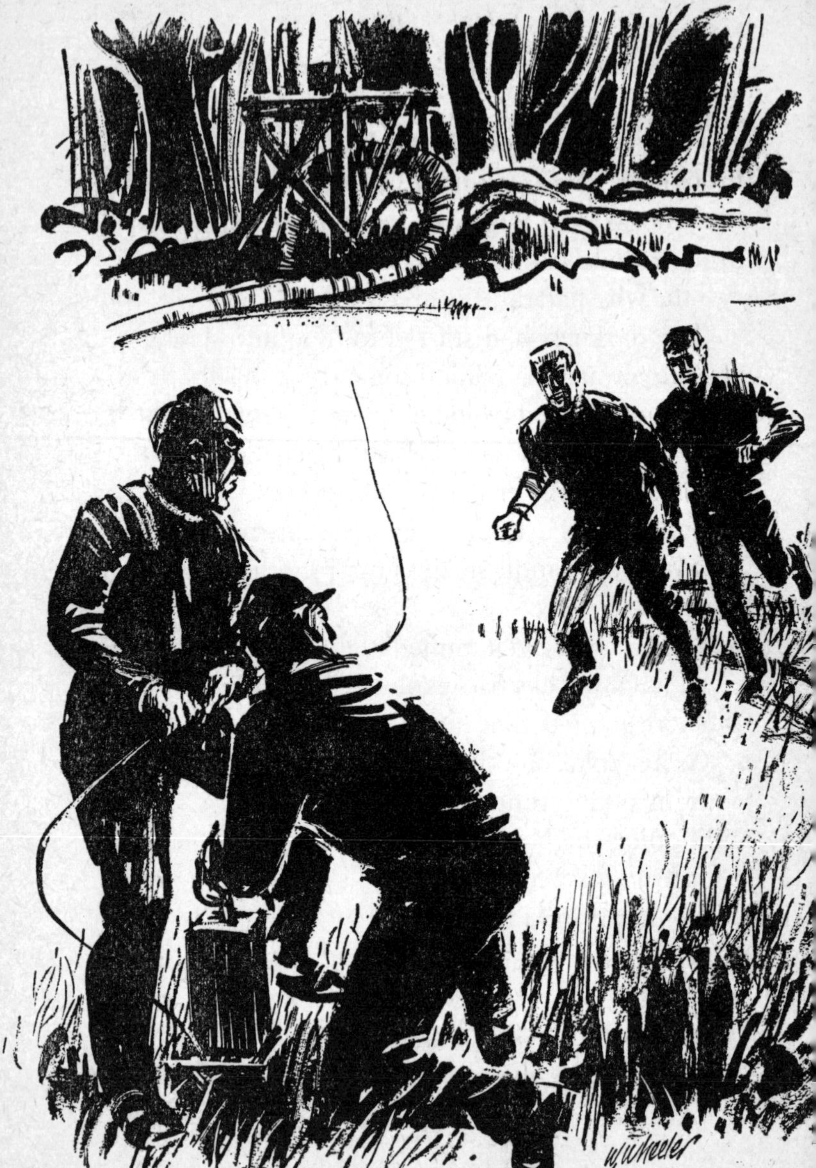
W.Wheeler

Dynamite 47

away from the box. That one second's delay was all the boy needed.

Rather than reach for the men, Brad threw himself toward the box and as he knocked the man away he fell heavily on his side. Grabbing the wires running into the box he yanked them clear.

With that, Brad rolled away trying to get to his feet.

He was too late!

The boy grunted as one of the dynamiters brought his full weight crashing down on his shoulders. Brad rolled as quickly as he could and managed to throw the man off.

Seizing one of the man's ankles, Brad twisted sharply, throwing his opponent to one side. Then cat-quick Brad leaped to his feet.

Before he could really get set another man raced in from the boy's right side with a pick raised high in the air. Ducking under the swinging pick, that would have dug its way into his skull, Brad grasped the handle with one hand. This stopped the force of the blow and then with the other hand Brad drove a judo chop hard into the crook's throat.

Dropping the pick the man grabbed his throat and started to fall to the ground gasping for breath.

Brad didn't wait to see what happened for the first attacker was charging again.

Bracing himself for the impact, Brad caught just

a glimpse from the corner of his eye as Conn was rolling his opponent on the ground.

"Whoosh!"

Brad met his rushing opponent with a powerful right fist that drove straight into the man's stomach. As the man doubled over Brad followed through with a left uppercut that snapped his head back. The glaze in the man's eye was enough to convince Brad he would be out of the fight for a long while to come.

The boy started to leap to his friend's assistance but he didn't make it. Captain Scott had arrived and was hauling Conn off.

"You sure made short work of those three," snapped the Captain.

"Glad you got here just the same," Brad panted.

"When I heard your yell I knew there was trouble. Let's get these three on their feet and back to the camp."

While Conn watched the men closely, Brad and Captain Scott herded them back past the dig toward the camp.

On the way they stopped long enough to pull the earth away from the ten dynamite sticks that were buried just alongside the excavation.

"Good work, Conn," said Captain Scott, when he pulled the wiring away from the caps. "This would have set us back for another month."

"I wonder why they wanted to blow the pit up?" asked Brad. "It seems a kind of stupid thing to do."

"We'll find out when we question them."

But though the Captain questioned the men carefully for an hour they found out little or nothing.

The three men were waterfront toughs from Halifax who'd been approached to do the job. They'd been given the equipment but none of them knew anything about the man who'd hired them.

"What's he look like?" snapped Scott.

"It was too dark to tell," one of the men snarled in reply.

"Where'd you meet this man?" asked Brad sharply.

"At a rooming house on Hamilton Street near the Halifax railroad station."

At this the crook Brad had chopped on the throat spoke up. "We were goin' to meet him tonight behind the government wharf in Chester and get paid if the job was done right."

"Hmmmm," said Brad.

Leaving Conn to watch the men, Brad motioned the Naval officer to one side.

"If they're supposed to meet the man who hired them tonight," he said quietly, "he must be somewhere nearby waiting for the explosion. He'd never pay them off without seeing something."

"That's true, Brad, but what can we do about it?"

"It might be our chance to trap him."

CHAPTER 7

Surprise Meeting

BRAD QUICKLY explained his plan and just as quickly Captain Scott approved.

"OKay, Brad, good idea! Let's get started."

While Conn kept his eye on the three prisoners, who seemed to have all the fight taken out of them, Brad and the Naval officer got to work.

First, they moved the dynamite three hundred yards away from the excavation. Carefully Brad replaced the wires on the end of five dynamite sticks and covered them with a loose pile of earth. On top of the earth he piled a heap of broken branches and then leading the wires from the pile to the battery exploder the boy had a quick look around to make sure everybody was clear of the area.

"All set, sir," the boy called.

"Let her go anytime, Brad."

Getting the explosion set off before it was too light was essential to their plan. If the man who was going to pay off the crooks was watching, the blast would have to come soon and be large enough for him to see from the mainland.

Watching the innocent looking pile of branches and earth, Brad slammed the plunger home and immediately the earth and branches erupted in a great, towering blast.

Even from this distance Brad could feel the ground tremble as the loose earth and branches reached high in the air above the oak trees.

"I hope he saw it, wherever he was," said Captain Scott when the dust had settled.

"So do I," said the boy, fervently.

The noise of the blast brought the workmen running from their tents to the site and without giving them too many details, Scott instructed three of them to guard the prisoners.

"I want to get back to Grey, now," he said to Brad. "When I take those three crooks into the Chester police I'll take Grey along at the same time."

Brad knew the Captain didn't want to talk about Grey and he didn't question him further. When they got to the tents the older man turned into his and then came running out again.

"Grey's gone!" he called.

"Gone?"

"Yes! He was sleeping when I left and I didn't

Surprise Meeting

think he could get away even if he did wake up."

"Gee," said Brad. "Just seeing Grey should make a good story and the circumstances should add lots of interest to it."

Captain Scott had turned back to his tent when Brad made this remark. Abruptly he stopped, then swung around to the boy.

For a few moments he studied Brad as though he wondered if he was trustworthy.

"You can't write that story, Brad," he said.

"I can't!" Brad cried. "Why?"

"I can't give you any details right now but for the next couple of days you've got to trust me. Write all you want about the money pit and the troubles we are having getting down to the treasure but you can't mention Grey or the people trying to delay us."

Brad knew enough about the newspaper business to know Captain Scott couldn't stop him from writing any kind of a story he wanted to. He also knew, however, that if he wrote the story now any chance of getting much information in the future would disappear. This was one of the times he would be smart to write nothing.

"OKay, sir," he said quietly. "I know there's something going on down here more important than the treasure. I'll wait until you're ready to release the complete story."

Captain Scott breathed a sigh of relief. "Thanks, Brad," he said. "You won't regret it."

Brad hoped he wouldn't. He also hoped that when the story broke he would get the first priority on the details.

"What do we do now?" the boy asked the tall Naval officer.

"All we can do is work out the day right here. I don't want to take those three crooks ashore until after dark. If we're being watched the man they're to meet would know something was wrong with his plan and he wouldn't show up."

"OKay," the boy agreed.

Brad spent the rest of the day helping Conn with the supplies. The cheery young fisherman kept up a running comment about the Nova Scotia coastline and the Mahone Bay area particularly. Brad knew all this information would make ideal background for the story he hoped to be able to write before too long.

"What do the people on the mainland think of all the activity on Oak Island?" Brad asked.

"They're used to it. The Navy has some kind of a big ammunition dump or somethin' underground on Grandall Point, the closest spot on the mainland from Oak Island."

"I didn't know that," said Brad.

"Not many people do. None of the people who work there live in Chester. They all go back and

Surprise Meeting 55

forth to Halifax in buses. But there's somethin' underground there and the locals just stay away."

After supper Brad wrote his notes on the feature story about Conn and then, with Captain Scott, they gathered the dynamiters together and took them ashore.

Captain Scott had been very skilful in questioning the crooks and he knew they were to make contact with their employer on the corner just behind the Government Wharf fish houses.

"All they know is that it's to be just after dark," said Scott when they'd delivered the crooks to the local police.

Conn, Brad and Captain Scott walked down the silent, darkened streets of Chester and, splitting up, they each eased back into a doorway.

"No rough stuff if it can be avoided," the Captain ordered.

Brad waited for an hour. He could see both the Captain and Conn stirring in the shadows but there was no sign of a stranger. Several times cars filled with people passed the corner but they didn't stop and didn't pay any attention to the spot.

Brad had begun to think their trap had failed to work. Then, from down the street, to his left, he heard quick footsteps pounding on the sidewalk.

Thinking this might be the man they were waiting for, the boy stepped out to the sidewalk and waited at the darkened corner of the building.

He could see the figure hurrying down the street toward them and then it stepped into the dim light from a street lamp.

Brad gasped in surprise.

It was Dwight Davis!

CHAPTER 8

New Operators

Brad knew his jaw dropped in surprise but he tried to control the expression on his face as well as he could. There were lots of suspicious things about Davis but even if he was the leader of a gang, the boy hardly expected him to appear in person.

"Good evening, Brad," Davis said. "Were you hiding there or were you just out for a stroll?"

Brad recovered himself quickly. "Just out for a stroll, sir."

Davis smiled graciously. "So was I. Lovely night for a walk, isn't it?"

Brad wanted to know how long the yachtsman had been ashore but before he could frame the question, Davis spoke up again.

"I'm heading back for 'Esther' now, have you got your own boat or could I drop you off on the island?"

"Thank you, Mr. Davis," said Brad. "I've got a

boat and I'm not thinking of going back right now anyway."

"All right, son, enjoy yourself." With that remark and a gay wave of his hand Dwight Davis turned and walked down toward the Government Wharf.

Brad watched him go, astounded. If he had been the contact the dynamiters were expecting, he was the most composed crook the boy could imagine. And, if he was innocent, meeting him here at this time was an amazing coincidence.

When Davis had turned the corner at the end of the street, Scott and Conn joined the boy.

"What was that all about?" the Captain asked, anxiously.

Brad explained and even the Naval officer had no explanation.

"I guess that's it," he said finally. "If Davis was the man those crooks were supposed to meet, he's fooled us for tonight and if he wasn't, it's probably too late for the payoff man anyway."

"Yeh," said Brad. "I suppose the best thing is for us to go back to Oak Island."

The three friends were silent on the way across Mahone Bay. Brad had been thinking more and more about Peter Grey, Davis, the payoff that didn't take place and the secret naval installation Conn had told him about.

New Operators 59

When they got back to the island his curiosity got the better of him.

"Conn told me there was some sort of secret naval installation ashore near here." Then he asked the captain, "Would that have anything to do with Peter Grey appearing and with the attempt to get you off Oak Island?"

Captain Scott thought for a moment before he spoke. Then he nodded. "It has everything to do with it," he said. "You must be imagining all kinds of things. The best thing is for me to tell you what I can and then maybe you can help."

Brad leaned forward eagerly. He hoped some of the suspicions racing through his mind would be cleared up.

"Even though I've been interested in the Oak Island treasure for years," began Scott, "I'm down here right now to do more than just dig for it. Though I'd like to solve the mystery of the treasure there's another mystery that's more important."

"What's that, sir?" Brad asked politely.

Scott lifted his hand to stop any further questions. "About three months ago the Naval Intelligence Department had some information from the NATO intelligence forces working out of Norfolk, Virginia, that something was to happen, shortly, to the underground installations at Grandall Point."

"You mean blow up the dump?" asked Conn.

Scott smiled. "It's not an ammunition dump,

Conn, though we've done everything we can to make the people around Chester believe it is. Buried underground at Grandall Point is an installation that's the only kind in the world and even though it's still in the experimental stage we hope it will be the first in a link of stations stretching from Florida to Greenland."

"Wow!" cried Conn.

"What kind of a station?" asked Brad.

"Right now I'm not at liberty to tell you exactly and anyway I don't know enough about the technical aspects to give you much more than the general idea. Anyway, the place is vital to the NATO defence of North America and for an agent of a foreign power to do anything to interfere with its operation would be a disaster."

"Do you work for Navy Intelligence?" asked Brad.

"Exactly. And so does Peter Grey."

"Grey?" the boy cried.

"He is one of the best men I have. The publicity about his dishonourable release from the Navy was kept vague and confusing for a purpose. All the charges were trumped up. All we wanted to do was put him in a position where his reputation would be bad enough the people trying to find out about Grandall Point would contact him."

"Did they?" asked Brad, eagerly.

"They did. Grey isn't as sure of his facts as he

New Operators

could be, but yesterday he told me he'd been swimming out in the bay to have a look at the keel on Davis' yacht. He didn't really know what he expected to find and as it turned out there was nothing."

"Then they did spot him," said Brad.

"That's right. It must have been just after we left 'Esther' and when they shot at him they probably thought he was killed or hurt. But they weren't that convinced because either Davis or Davis' gang landed and took him out of my tent while I was with you or he left of his own accord and I can't believe that."

"Why not, sir?"

"We weren't nearly through with our conversation. I wanted to give him lots of instructions about what to do next. He's a member of Davis' gang, even though he hasn't been aboard 'Esther' yet. He's been working out of Halifax and that's probably where you and Conn can help us out."

"I love a mystery!" said Conn, grinning.

"This is no joke," said Scott, seriously. "Somebody has to go down and have a look around the house on Hamilton Street where Peter and the men in Halifax are staying. I could organize a raid on the place but even if we did capture a half dozen men it wouldn't prove anything. I have to know exactly what they're planning to do here in Mahone Bay."

"Is that where Conn and I come in?" asked Brad.

"That's it. But only if you want to, of course. It could be dangerous but if you could find out anything at all it might help the country more than you'll ever know."

"Not only that," thought Brad, "but it will help with my story."

"What do you think, Conn?" Brad asked aloud.

Conn scratched his head. "I don't care," he said, cheerfully. "I'm always ready for anythin'."

Brad turned to the Naval officer.

"OKay, Captain. You've got yourself a couple of new operators."

CHAPTER 9

17 Hamilton Street

The next evening, just after dark, two roughly dressed young men, looking like many merchant sailors around Halifax, turned off Barrington Street into Hamilton Street.

They had been walking up and down Halifax's main street for an hour, idly gazing in the store windows. Twice they had walked the short length of Hamilton Street and though nobody noticed, each time they looked carefully at the front door of number 17.

The tough-looking sailors were Brad Forrest and Conn Casey.

Before the boys had left Oak Island, Brad had changed into a pair of dungarees and a turtle neck sweater belonging to Conn. Then, after Captain Scott had warned them again about being careful, he gave them a telephone number in Halifax to call if they got into trouble.

"Remember," he said, when they were just about to climb into the bus for Halifax, "I just want you to have a look around that house on Hamilton Street. If you manage to talk to any of the people living there, or overhear anything they might say, that's fine. But let me warn you again this gang is made up of international experts and they would just as soon kill you as look at you."

The lights on Hamilton Street were far apart and dim enough to just barely illuminate the front doors of the rooming houses and small, sleezy hotels lining it. Each of the houses seemed to have its own small front yard and between each one was a high board fence hiding what Brad thought must be a back yard.

Though most of the houses were in darkness there was just a trace of light coming from the heavily curtained windows of number 17.

"There must be somebody in there," said Brad, as the boys walked past the place for the third time.

"That's right. But we can walk up and down here all night and we'll never get the information Captain Scott wants."

Brad remembered the Naval officer's caution and he didn't want to walk right up to the front door and ask for a room.

"Why not?" asked Conn.

"For one thing," Brad replied, "even though most of the places have a sign in the window saying they have rooms for rent this one hasn't. They're sure to be suspicious of two strangers that walk in the front door."

"How about the back door?" asked Conn.

"Why not!" Brad cried. "That could just be the answer. Even if we didn't get in we might manage to hear something."

The boys waited for a few minutes until the street was deserted and then, moving like wraiths, they nipped over the high board fence and jumped down into the total darkness of the back yard.

Underfoot they could feel the collection of broken bottles and rough stones that filled the yard. Careful as they were, each time they moved, there was a rattle from the stones and bottles.

When his eyes got used to the blackness, Brad motioned ahead to his friend. They saw they were close enough to a small back porch to climb up and over the railing.

"C-r-e-a-k!" Brad stood still as the railing squeaked under his weight.

"Squeeze under it," Brad whispered to his friend.

Conn did and in a second the boys were standing together in front of a wooden door leading into the back of the house.

"We're not going to find nothin' here," whispered Conn.

Brad agreed. The door looked as though it

hadn't been opened for years and there wasn't a sign of light from the two windows they could see.

"Let's see if the door'll open," Brad said.

Working slowly and together the boys grasped the old-fashioned handle and pulled the door toward them.

It stuck for a second then eased open silently revealing a corridor ahead that looked just like a black, underground cave.

Brad walked ahead, sliding one foot after the other. From behind, Conn kept his hand on the boy's shoulder and moved as silently as he could. Inside the house there was quiet and not a sign of light.

Brad had moved ahead about three paces when he felt one of the boards underfoot move slightly. He wouldn't have been surprised if he'd fallen right through, the house was so old and so musty.

Suddenly Brad felt his right elbow brush something solid. Reaching out into the darkness his palm touched a wall.

"There's a wall here," he whispered over his shoulder. "If we move down it we should come to a door."

"Keep goin', Brad! This place gets me!"

Brad moved ahead two more steps and then in front of him the blackness was shattered as a door crashed open and the corridor was flooded with light.

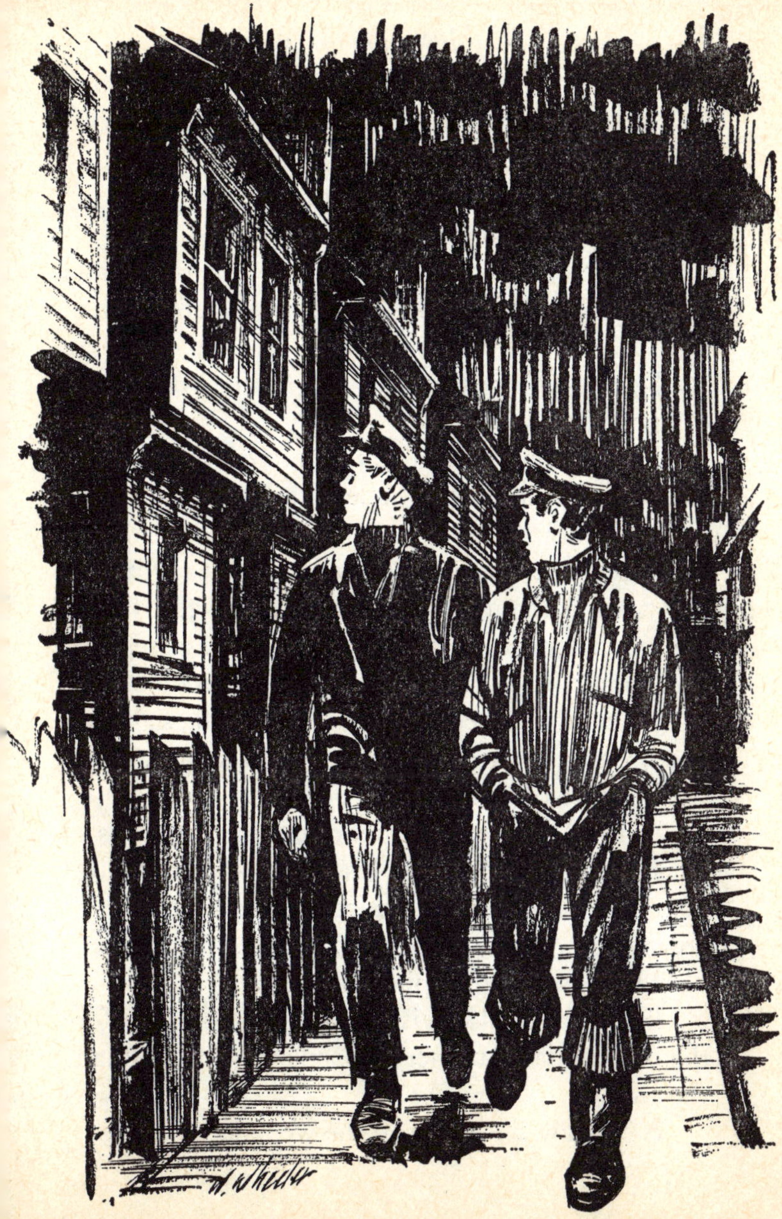

Sucking in his breath with surprise, the boy turned ready to run for the back door. As he turned the rest of the lights in the corridor flashed on and three men charged them from the open door.

"Back!" yelled Conn.

But he was too late! Another door they had missed burst open and from it came three more men.

The boys were trapped! But neither Brad nor Conn would give up.

Turning on his heel Brad charged toward the back door hoping to bowl one of the men off his feet and get out that way.

Swinging a power house right, Brad caught the first crook flush on the jaw. The man staggered into the one behind him and with a yell and a mighty leap Brad cleared the huddle of bodies on the floor.

When he glanced over his shoulder the sight he saw brought his heart leaping into his mouth.

Conn was down!

As Brad glanced, his friend stumbled again as a second thug leaped on his back and swinging high over his shoulder brought a blackjack crashing down on the young fisherman's head.

The glance had trapped Brad too!

Before he could twist to one side and leap for the door he saw another weapon swinging through the air.

As he saw the swing of the weapon he thought

there was a familiar face among the group of men around the fallen Conn.

He felt for an instant as though the back of his head was going to explode.

Then in a burst of light he lost consciousness!

CHAPTER 10

"Le Grand"

BRAD WOKE with something hard and sharp digging into his back.

Because he was in perfect health, the boy recovered his wits quickly. Under the back of his head he could feel he was lying on a steel floor of some kind and when he opened his eyes he saw the whole room was steel.

Swinging to his feet, a quick glance told him he and Conn were in a ship's cabin. There were two bright lights on the deckhead and two bunks welded to one of the bulkheads, just beyond the bunks he could see the dirty brass ring of a scuttle and the darkness beyond.

How was Conn?

This was more important than where they were now!

Brad leaned over the boy and could see an ugly yellow bruise on his right temple. The boy lifted his friend's head away from the deck and this was just enough to make Conn stir.

The young Nova Scotian opened his eyes and with Brad's help sat up. Raising one hand to the bruise he rubbed it carefully.

When he grinned, Brad knew he wasn't badly hurt. "I guess goin' to the back door wasn't such a good idea after all," he said, ruefully.

"Guess not," said Brad. "It was my fault we were trapped, though. When that old-looking back door opened so quietly I should have known it was oiled and had been used before. Then when one of the boards moved that must have been a signal we were coming in."

"Don't worry about it now," said Conn, getting to his feet. "Where are we anyway?"

While Conn went over to look from the scuttle, Brad tried the door. There were eight clips holding it tight in place but he easily twisted those back. But the door still wouldn't open.

"It must be locked on the outside," the boy thought.

"We're on a ship in Bedford Basin!" cried Conn from the porthole.

"Bedford Basin!" exclaimed Brad, joining Conn at the port.

"Yeh, look!"

By twisting himself from side to side, Brad could

just see the sweep of the Bedford Basin shore and the lights of cars moving down the highway.

Conn twisted furiously at the clips holding the scuttle in place but it was no use. Each of them had been welded to the bulkhead.

"The door's secured too," said Brad.

Together the boys sank down side by side on the springs of one of the rough bunks.

They were in a prison that was sure to hold them tight.

"Whatta we do now, Brad?" asked Conn, slowly.

"There's not much we can do but wait for the next move. Captain Scott won't have any idea where we are. He'll just think we've vanished."

The boys sat despondently on the bunks for a half hour trying to figure a way out of the steel cabin or a way they could signal somebody ashore but nothing they thought of was any good unless they got out of the cabin.

After a brooding silence, Conn suddenly sprang to his feet.

"What's that?" he gasped.

Brad didn't answer for a minute but he too could feel the movement in the deck under their feet and hear a rumble that seemed to come from the forward end of the ship.

"We're getting under way!" Brad cried.

"That's it! If we're still on board when this

"Le Grand"

ship gets out of Halifax harbour we'll be in a real peck of trouble."

Conn ran to the door and twisted the clips around in circles. Nothing happened for a minute and then suddenly the door was yanked open.

Standing at the door was a tough-looking sailor who was wearing a pistol in his belt and a snarl on his face.

"Dat won't do you no good," he sneered. "You're goin' on a trip now whether you like it or not."

"Where are ..." Brad didn't get a chance to finish his sentence when the door was slammed shut and as they were moved from the outside the boys could see the door-clips fall in place.

"Nice fellow," snapped Brad.

"Huh!" was all Conn could say.

By this time the movement in the ship's deck was easy to feel. Brad knew the rumble they heard was the anchor chain coming in through the hawse pipe and the movement was the vibration from the ship's main engines as they turned over.

Crowding together, Brad and Conn could look out of the port and the Nova Scotian could identify the spots the ship passed as they went out of the Basin and started to move into Bedford Narrows.

"There's the Naval Magazine," said Conn, and then, "there's the dockyard."

In a moment the lights of the downtown part of

the city itself came into view, then the huge warehouses near the main commercial docks.

When they passed the yacht club, Point Pleasant and then Sandwich Point, Conn left the port and sat down on the bunk again.

"We're goin' to sea for sure, now," he said.

With that remark, Brad felt the first heave as the heavy Atlantic rollers caught the ship and it started to pitch slightly.

Brad never knew how long they waited, sitting on the bunk, until finally out of the corner of his eye, near the door, he caught the slightest motion. Quickly he nudged his friend to get his attention.

As they watched, the clips on the door moved slowly, one after the other. As the last one dropped into a vertical position it jerked up and down. It almost looked as though whoever was moving it on the other side of the door was trying to catch their attention.

"Maybe we can get him when he comes in," whispered Brad.

Together the friends leaped to their feet and tiptoed across to the door. Conn stood ready to yank the door open as soon as it started to move and Brad was set to attack the first person stepping into the cabin.

The clips stopped moving and they waited. But nothing happened. Muscles tensed and with his breath coming in short gasps Brad waited—and waited. Still nothing happened.

Brad glanced at Conn and then the boy reached out for the handle to see if the door would open.

"Just a minute!" Conn stopped Brad by grabbing his arm.

Conn dashed over to the porthole and looked out. Wondering what was going on Brad joined him.

"What's the matter?" he hissed urgently.

"If that door's open," replied Conn, "we might just be able to get up on deck and over the side. There wouldn't be any use makin' a try for it until we had a chance of being picked up."

Conn stared through the darkness looking for something he could recognize.

"There it is!" he said finally. "Look, Brad!" he pointed.

By pressing his face close to the heavy glass Brad could see a flashing light ahead of them.

"That's the light on Prospect Point," snapped Conn. "At least I hope it is."

"Where's that?"

"Just outside of Halifax and a quick turn to the west," explained Conn. "If we keep goin' in this direction we'll be close to Peggy's Cove in a few minutes."

"Then what?"

Conn laughed. "Then, if that door's open, we

should see some of the boys in their dorys and we could take a chance on goin' over the side."

Eagerly the two friends watched and finally Conn said quietly, "There they are."

Quite close to the ship's side Brad could see several winking lights that were close to the water. They were bobbing up and down with the movement of the waves and were spread out right to the shore where there were the dim lights of the houses.

"Let's go now!" Conn snapped.

Together the boys sped to the door and then very carefully tried it.

It was open!

Outside was a small corridor of the type that's known in a ship as a flat and on the port side was a ladder leading up to the deck.

Conn was first up the ladder with Brad close behind.

When the boys broke into the night air, Brad could see they had been held prisoner in the stern of the ship.

He paused for a look around but Conn grabbed his arm and pointed to the rail and then at the two men who were standing well forward on the deck beside an open hatch and staring back at them.

"Hurry, Brad!" Conn snapped.

Together the boys rushed down the few steps to the main part of the deck and ran toward the rail.

They heard the men yell and knew they'd been spotted.

As Brad passed the uncovered hatch he glanced down and saw a huge saucer-shaped collection of aluminum and wire that looked like a radar antennae.

There was no time to stop now!

The crooks from the ship were shouting and rushing back toward them.

Along the deck at the bottom of the rail was a heavy coil of wire that Brad thought must have been about three feet in diameter.

Stepping on the coil Brad climbed the ship's rail just as one of the men was reaching for him.

Then he leaped after Conn into the black waters of the Atlantic Ocean.

CHAPTER 11

Into the Ocean

When he dove, Brad saw Conn's heels just disappearing in the waves and he heard the shouts of the men behind him.

He knew the water would be cold but he hadn't been prepared for the icy shock that took his breath away. Surfacing as quickly as he could, Brad saw Conn was just ahead of him and to the right.

When he saw Conn was all right, the first thing that darted into his mind was the suction. He knew they must get as far away from the ship's side as possible. There was no danger of the ship turning into them in such a short distance but there was real danger they would be sucked into the powerful propellers that would cut them to bits.

In spite of the clothes he was wearing and the shoes on his feet, Brad Forrest never swam as hard or as fast as he did now.

From the churning of the water ahead, he knew

Into the Ocean

Conn was thinking of the same thing. Right now they didn't think about swimming toward one of the twinkling lights that were ahead and close to the surface.

They just wanted to get away from the ship!

Weighted down by the heavy clothes, Brad could maintain this furious pace for just a few minutes. Sucking in a great draught of air he knew he would have to stop and tread water, but somehow he had to keep going just a little longer.

At the finish of one last burst of speed and effort the boy's hand crashed into something in the water and abruptly he stopped swimming.

It was Conn!

"OKay, Brad!" panted his friend.

Gratefully Brad let his feet drop down and allowed his body to relax. With Conn he looked back towards the brightly lit ship they had just left and watched it slide away into the darkness. On deck were at least a dozen men running back and forth pointing toward them.

As the full flush of the stern slid past Brad could see the ship's name and the port of registry. "Le Grand" was the name and under it the word "Istanbul".

It flashed through the boy's mind that the ship's name was familiar for some reason but right now he had more important things to think about.

Where were the dorys?

As Brad swung away from the direction of the ship he thought, for an instant, they'd all disappeared. But they hadn't. When the boy looked he'd been deep in the trough of an Atlantic wave and had seen nothing but the steep sides of another.

When he rose to the crest Brad could see both Conn and, just ahead of him, the lights of the dorys.

"Common!" yelled Conn.

The boys swam hard for the lights and in a few minutes were hauled into one of the double-ended boats like two exhausted cod fish.

Conn knew the two men in the boat and though they asked lots of questions he dodged them skilfully by making a joke of the whole affair.

"All we need to do, boys, is to get into Peggy's Cove as quickly as we can," said Conn. "Someday I'll tell you all about it."

The dorymen stripped off their jackets and gave them to the boys and while Brad and Conn shivered in the boat's bottom the oars were shipped and an outboard motor rigged on the stern.

Though Brad had nearly lost his sense of direction completely, the dorymen seemed to be able to see in the dark. When the boat leaped ahead for the shore Brad raised himself enough to look over the gunwales at the fading lights of the ship that'd held them prisoner.

Ahead and off to the left, he could see the North

Into the Ocean

Star off the end of the Big Dipper's handle. "Le Grand" had disappeared in the general direction of the North Star and just a bit to the left of it. Brad knew then her course would be almost due northwest.

Just as he knew so many fishermen on the coast, Conn knew the owner of the tiny general store at Peggy's Cove. He let Brad use his telephone to call the number in Halifax Captain Scott had given them, then, very kindly, insisted they dry their clothes while they waited for the Navy car.

"A car will be there to pick you up in less than an hour," the officer on the telephone had said when the boy explained who he was and that he urgently needed to see Captain Scott.

The young Naval officer who arrived to pick up the boys was tight lipped and quiet. He asked no questions and neither Brad nor Conn supplied him with any information. The car sped along the coast toward Mahone Bay, being driven as fast as safety would allow, and Scott, with his boat, was waiting for them at the Government Wharf in Chester.

He dismissed the officer who had brought them from Peggy's Cove and even kept his own questions until they were back in his tent on Oak Island, each boy wolfing down sandwiches.

Between bites, Brad explained all that had happened. When he got to the point of thinking one of the men who'd attacked Conn was familiar, Scott stopped him.

"Familiar?" he queried.

"Yes, sir," affirmed Brad, "but I just got a glance at him."

"Could it have been Peter Grey?"

"G-o-l-l-e-e-," said Brad, thinking about the question. "It could have been. If he's managed to get back in the gang without arousing suspicion he could have been the man who took the clips off the cabin door and let us get away."

"That's what I thought," snapped the Captain. "Grey hasn't managed to leave any kind of word for me at all. What we need to know is where 'Le Grand' was going."

"The last we saw of her she was heading northwest," Brad said.

Scott leaped to his feet and spread out a chart of the coast from Halifax to Cape Sable. Pointing to a spot he said, "This must have been about where you jumped and if the ship was heading northwest it's not going out to sea."

"What does that mean?" Conn asked slowly.

"Common, boys!" said Scott, moving toward the tent's entrance. "It might mean we can still get our hands on it before it gets beyond the twelve mile limit."

Scott hurried them across the island and through the darkness toward the southeast part near where the power line crossed to Grandall Point. With no explanations he urged them into an outboard motor boat and they crossed the short stretch of the Bay over to the point.

Landing on a deserted strip of the beach, near some thick undergrowth, they were just climbing out of the boat when an armed sentry stopped them.

Scott had a few urgent, low words with him and then showed a special pass he took from his wallet.

Though Brad couldn't see the man clearly, the boy thought he was in some kind of uniform. As Brad and Conn followed the tall Naval officer through the thick undergrowth he wondered where they were going and what kind of an installation the Navy could have here.

When he found out his eyes goggled!

CHAPTER 12

Ops Room

THERE WAS an entrance to the underground operations room beneath a bush that didn't seem large enough to conceal the metal ladder leading ten steps below to a steel-walled room.

Captain Scott knew exactly what he was doing as he reached out and pressed a button hidden in one of the bolts that held a steel plate to the wall.

From straight ahead of them a shiny panel slid to one side and they stepped into an elevator that dropped them at least one hundred feet underground.

From the elevator they stepped straight into the operations room itself.

The walls of the room were huge and concave in shape. Just ahead of the three friends were a maze of desks with large, light green radar screens facing them.

There were five Naval officers sitting at the

desks and on the wall facing them was an enormous map covering an area of the Atlantic seaboard from Cape Farewell to Bermuda. The map must have been electronically controlled for it was thick with tiny red and green lights, some flashing and some that seemed to be standing still. Beside each was a letter and a number.

All of the radar screens in front of the watch-keeping officers, except one, were glowing in the softened light. On their surface were lines and figures Brad recognized as bearings and ranges and on some of the lines were large grey-green blobs.

All of the men working in the room were going quietly about their business, in spite of the constant chatter of the teletype machines.

Captain Scott didn't give the boys any time for sight seeing. He urged them across the room until they stood behind the desk with the blank radar screen in front of it.

Quickly Scott introduced the boys to Lieutenant Commander Jordan. "You remember I told you these young men were helping me out with the case I've been working on," he said.

When Lieutenant Commander Jordan nodded, Scott explained about "Le Grand" and what had happened to them.

"The ship should be close into Mahone Bay now," Scott finished, "if she maintained the course she was on when Brad and Conn went swimming.

If she did, we can still have a destroyer pick her up."

"Let's have a look at the short range set," said Lieutenant Commander Jordan.

With Scott and the boys close behind, he crossed the room with long strides and spoke to one of the junior officers behind a desk.

"Switch on, Harmon," he ordered.

The officer made some swift adjustments on the set and the grey-green blobs seemed to take on some kind of definite shape. Behind each was a purple line.

For a second, Jordan studied the set and then, shaking his head, he turned to Captain Scott.

"There's nothing, sir. Those purple lines are the courses those ships have taken since they came within a fifty mile range of this station and nothing has come down from Peggy's Cove tonight."

"That means he's turned out to sea? How about the long range sets?"

"Right here." When Jordan answered he switched on another group of radar sets. "There's nothing, sir. Each of these ships has been accounted for and each is just about in the position they should be. That ship isn't within a thousand miles of this station."

"What can that mean?" asked Brad, puzzled. " 'Le Grand' just couldn't have disappeared."

"Could she have slipped into the coast close

enough for you not to be able to make contact with her?" Scott asked Jordan.

"Not a chance, sir. These sets are so sensitive we can pick out the lobster fishermen heading for their pots. Some of the operators say that when conditions are at their best you can even pick out the flags on the lobster buoys."

When Lieutenant Commander Jordan finished speaking he studied both Brad and Conn for a minute and then looked at Captain Scott.

Scott frowned. "I know what you're thinking, Jordan, but it certainly isn't a case of an overworked imagination. Don't forget I know both of these young men."

"Sorry, sir," said Jordan quietly. "There is something else we might try but I don't think it's much use."

Back at his own desk, Jordan switched on the darkened set and quickly adjusted it. This set was small enough to be completely portable.

"This is the most hush-hush piece of radar equipment in the world," he said firmly. "I'm sure I don't have to tell you how important it is, sir."

"No you don't," snapped Captain Scott, "and you don't have to worry about my two friends here, either."

Jordan nodded and then, reaching out, touched a small button on the set's side. For a second Brad had trouble recognizing the lines that appeared like magic.

"This is called a 'Radar Profile Indicator' and it's been developed from a wartime gadget called an IFF."

"What was that?" Brad asked eagerly.

"IFF is short for 'Information Friend or Foe' and it was a machine that told a ship or an aircraft if a radar target was friend or enemy. This machine goes one step farther, it actually supplies you with a profile—an outline of the ship or the aircraft."

As he talked, Jordan pressed another button and the picture on the screen started to move backwards and forwards. At each jumble of lines it paused and they quickly became an outline of a ship. So clear were they that Brad thought for a second the profiles must have been three dimensional.

"That's a tanker," said Scott, pointing, "and that's a private steam yacht; you can see they are flying a flag from the mainmast and one of their aerials is slack."

Brad stared at the lines, hardly able to believe the yacht whose outline he saw was 100 miles southeast of Cape Sable, the very southernmost tip of Nova Scotia.

Watching, they saw the "Radar Profile Indicator" click from contact to contact and each of them leaped into perfect outline.

None of them had the old-fashioned, three-island construction of "Le Grand".

"That's all we can do, sir," said Jordan, finally. "If the ship you're looking for is anywhere in our area it must have sunk."

Captain Scott stood staring at the complicated radar set for a long minute. He rubbed his chin as he thought and then said, "There's something going on here we have to find out about, right now. Keep a good lookout for anything you can't understand. I'm going back to Halifax to talk to some of the Navy electronic experts."

"Right, sir!" Lieutenant Commander Jordan acknowledged the order. "I'm sorry I couldn't help you."

"Let's go, boys," ordered Scott.

When Captain Scott and the boys came out of the buried ops room and stepped into the thick undergrowth on Grandall Point, Brad rubbed his eyes. He could hardly believe they were so close to such a complicated and secret installation.

Escorted by the alert sentry who had met them when they stepped ashore, Captain Scott led the way back to the small boat with the outboard.

After they climbed on board and got the motor started the Captain headed the boat around the southern tip of Oak Island and toward the town of Chester.

"I've got a car in Chester," he said. "I'll get

down to Halifax as quickly as possible and try and get back tonight or tomorrow. I'd like you boys to get back to Oak Island and keep the dig running as normally as possible."

"Any special instructions?" Brad asked.

"I don't think so. Just keep the men working and keep yourselves in sight. If Davis is connected with what's going on around here he'll have somebody watching the island and it might be a good thing to let him see you around."

When Captain Scott left, Brad and Conn stopped at one of the small restaurants and ate a hearty breakfast. Without wasting time they headed back for the wharf and their boat. They wanted to get back to the dig before the sun got too far up.

When the boys turned the corner of the street leading down to the wharf they nearly bumped into a man hurrying into town.

It was Dwight Davis!

CHAPTER 13

Fog

BRAD WAS surprised to see Davis but he wasn't prepared for the shock Davis showed.

The older man stopped dead on the street. His mouth fell open and his eyebrows flew up.

Staring at the boy, as though he was a ghost, Davis opened his mouth to speak and though his lips moved not a sound came out.

Finally he managed some words. "Br . . . uh . . . Br . . . ."

He swallowed quickly twice more, then cried, "Brad Forrest! What are you doing here?"

"I just came ashore on an errand for Captain Scott," Brad said carefully. "Isn't it kind of early for you to be up and about, Mr. Davis?"

Brad's words gave the older man just time to compose himself and when he spoke again he was the self-assured yachtsman Brad had met before.

"Yes," he said cheerily, "but I thought it would

be a nice morning to stretch my legs. I was going to come over to Oak Island but I didn't think you would have had breakfast yet."

Brad smiled. The confidence Davis was showing didn't fool the boy for a second. When Davis' mask had been stripped away Brad knew the other man had thought he should be dead instead of walking the streets of Chester.

"Well," said Davis, waving his hand, "I'll get on with my walk now."

Both Brad and Conn turned to watch Davis hurry up the street toward the centre of town.

"What do you think of that?" Brad asked.

Conn scratched his head. "I don't know what to think except he sure didn't expect to bump into us."

"Are you thinking what I am, Conn?"

"Sure am! Davis knew we were on that ship and thought we'd be nothin' else but lobster bait by now."

In spite of their strange meeting with Dwight Davis the boys got back to Oak Island in time to get the work at the dig started.

The results of the sabotage had all been cleared out and for the rest of the day Brad helped the men fit the horizontal beams into place. They would prevent the sides from caving in again.

When they finished for the night, Brad and

Conn made sure the sentries knew what they had to do and then they took a walk around the island.

Conn showed Brad the two spots on the beach where the experts on the Oak Island treasure figured the tides flowed in and out of the hole.

"Nobody's been able to discover how it works," explained Conn. "A couple of years ago somebody dug down into the beach at both spots and discovered flat rocks used as tiles and an area lined with some kind of rushes that don't grow around here at all."

"Is that the only clue they have?"

"No it isn't. The same people pumped a whole lot of water coloured with dye into the hole and then came over here to the beach to see what would happen."

"What did happen?"

"The water came right through the whole system and when it flowed over the beach here it was still blue."

"I guess there's no doubt there really is a treasure," Brad observed.

"I don't know," Conn said, "my grandfather used to say that even if there wasn't a treasure somebody went to a lot of trouble to make sure whatever was in that hole was well hidden."

Reaching the island's west side the boys walked slowly down the narrow beach in the gathering darkness. Brad was tired and anxious to get to bed but he was still wondering about Captain Scott and when he'd get back.

When they were approaching the power line towers opposite Grandall Point Brad stopped and then looked at the high water mark on the beach.

"I wonder who uses this beach?" he said, half to himself.

"I dunno," Conn replied. "But somebody has been bringing boats on and off here a lot."

There were half a dozen keel marks along the shore and beside them many footprints dug into the sand. A group of men had been dragging some heavy boats right up on the beach and not too long before.

"I guess it can't be much," Brad said when they walked on toward the camp. When they ducked into the thick cluster of oak trees at the end of the island, Brad took the trouble to look back up the stretch of deserted beach. He couldn't imagine what troubled him but there was something out of place other than the unusual marks on the shore.

"The marks could have been made by anybody having a picnic out here," he thought.

Brad and Conn got to their tent and almost dismissed the mysterious marks from their minds. Conn stretched and yawned at the tent's entrance and then sniffed the air suspiciously.

"What's the matter?"

"There's some weather working up."

Fog

Brad looked up at the cloudless sky and pretended to listen to the quiet murmur of the wind.

"What kind of weather?" he asked with a smile.

"Bad weather," said Conn. "All of us fishermen can smell it, no matter what the forecast says."

"It'll take more than a hurricane to keep me awake tonight," muttered Brad, climbing into his sleeping bag.

"Just wait until tomorrow," laughed Conn, "you might see a change."

In the morning there was no change in the weather. The sun was as bright and the sky as cloudless as it had been the night before.

Brad kidded his friend about his weather predictions but Conn wouldn't be put off.

"Just wait," the Nova Scotian said.

Captain Scott arrived back in the middle of the afternoon and when the boys tied up the boat for him they were both full of questions.

"What did you find out?" Brad asked, eagerly.

"Not much! There's no doubt there was a ship in Halifax named 'Le Grand'. She put in there for repairs but wouldn't let anybody else but the harbour officials aboard. She was going to make her own repairs and they said none of the men were going ashore so the customs and immigration men didn't bother with her too much."

"Was she from Istanbul?"

"So the Captain told the pilot that took them

into the harbour but the ship's registry has no trace of the company that was supposed to be operating the ship."

"Did the Navy have any ideas on how she disappeared?" asked Brad.

"Not a one. In fact if they hadn't known the ship had sailed and that she wasn't on Lieutenant Commander Jordan's plot they would think we were dreaming."

When Captain Scott got up to his tent, he turned to the boys. "I've got to write up some reports. Are things at the dig going along OKay?"

"Sure they are."

"That's fine. Why don't you two take the rest of the day off. You must have some writing to do, Brad?"

"Thanks sir! I do."

"I'd like to go out and look at my lobster pots," Conn put in. "I'd better make sure they're all right before the weather blows up."

Captain Scott looked up at the sky and then down at Conn. "Your Nova Scotian nose itching?" he asked.

"I've been kidding him about it since yesterday," Brad laughed.

When Brad started back for his tent and his typewriter he looked up at the bright blue sky and couldn't face the thought of working, at least until that evening.

"Wait up, Conn!" he called, running after his friend. "It's about time I got a look at those pots of yours."

"Good! I'll be glad to have you."

"How far out do we go?" Brad asked, when Conn's dory had been puttering across Mahone Bay for nearly an hour.

"It'll be a way yet. The pots are all on a shoal between Heckman's Island and the Mahone Bay buoy."

The trip out to the mouth of the bay was fine but as the sun went down Brad noticed the clouds were gathering in the southwest, though the wind was coming from the east.

"Won't you have trouble finding your way back?" Brad asked, when Conn had finished checking the sixth pot.

"Nah. I've been comin' out here since I was smaller than a squid."

When Conn had finished his job and turned back for Oak Island the sun had just dropped over the horizon. Behind them Brad could see the fog rolling in and ahead the black clouds had risen to towering, swirling thunderheads.

CHAPTER 14

Missing Ship

THE THREATENING clouds, the fog and the darkness rushing in on them were beginning to worry Brad. All around the sea was leaping up in steep crests, breaking over the shoals then hurtling off for the shore line neither of them could see.

"Don't worry, Brad," Conn laughed. "I've been comin' out here at night for years. All we have to do is leave the Mahone Bay buoy to starboard and then head straight in."

Brad laughed too. He wasn't afraid but he didn't think there was any percentage being foolhardy in such a heavy sea.

As the dory leaped from crest to crest and the bow slammed into the water and then jumped for the next wave, Brad was amazed at how dry these little boats were. He'd heard about the Newfoundland fishermen spending days and nights in them on the Grand Banks far out from the shore. Though they seemed safe as an ocean liner and he trusted his Nova Scotian friend, Brad didn't think Conn should take any more chances with the uncertain weather.

"Here we go, Brad!" yelled Conn.

With that he swung the boat to port and then close down their starboard side passed the Mahone Bay buoy. From such a small boat and through the darkness the buoy looked as big as a ten-storey office building, its "bong" cutting through the darkness with an irregular beat.

Beyond the buoy was only darkness thickened by the fog that lay in patches tight down against the disturbed surface of the white-crested sea.

Brad thought Conn was like a homing pigeon the way he steered the boat straight into one of the thickest patches, knowing exactly the direction to Oak Island.

As far as Brad could tell the young fisherman didn't alter his course as much as a degree as the small boat bounced from trough to trough and then to another crest.

Perfectly dry, Brad sat in the dory's bow watching straight ahead through the dark greyness of the fog. He wondered for a moment if Conn would be able to find his way as easily when it was completely dark but his friend was sitting at the outboard motor whistling cheerily as it got darker and darker.

Brad could barely see twenty-five yards when in

the thick fog ahead he thought he saw a shape that looked solid.

Rubbing the fog from his eyes he looked again. There was nothing for a second and then the shape, darker than the fog behind it, appeared again. For just a second the shape passed through a thinner part of the fog bank and distinctly Brad saw the after part of a ship.

The after deck was low with the poop hanging behind and though he looked and looked there wasn't a sign of a light.

Then he recognized it!

"It's 'Le Grand'," he yelled. "Look, Conn. It's 'Le Grand'!"

"I see it! Don't lose sight of it!"

Turning for just an instant, Conn twisted a knob on the outboard. Brad heard the motor speed up and then felt the boat surge ahead at an even greater speed.

Even as the boat moved, "Le Grand" disappeared.

"Watch the spot!" Conn screamed over the roar of the motor and the howl of the wind.

Brad kept his eyes glued to the spot in the fog bank where the ship had disappeared as Conn steered straight for it. As the dory bounced over the sea, through the fog that seemed to thicken and thin out so quickly, Brad strained his eyes for a sight of the familiar hull.

Missing Ship

Several times the boy thought he saw something but each time when Conn turned the dory toward the spot there was nothing there.

They zigged and zagged back and forth but found only more fog. It seemed as though "Le Grand" had once again disappeared from the surface of the ocean.

"It's no use!" Conn shouted, cutting the boat's speed. "He's gotten away! He must have been doing twenty knots to do it."

"Don't slow down, Conn," Brad urged. "Let's get back to the island and tell the Captain."

"OKay! But it's going to be a wet trip!"

Conn pushed the dory's throttle wide open again and Brad crouched in the bows as the boat headed just a degree or two off the head sea.

The dory had been fine and dry when they were meeting the sea straight on but by just steering a trifle away from it the cold waves splattered on the blunt bow and sprayed right into the boat.

In a second Brad was soaked. He wondered if there was any danger of the boat being swamped but it didn't take long for him to notice that though there was lots of spray flying over the boat the design kept even the smallest waves from coming aboard.

After what seemed to Brad like hours, they passed under the shelter of Indian Point and the sea flattened out. The wind was still strong and the fog thick but the ride in the dory was dryer if not more comfortable.

Finally, after darkness had fallen completely and Brad had begun to think they were lost, Conn called out, "You should see some lights ahead on Oak Island in just a minute."

Brad strained his eyes looking into the thick blackness ahead and then, as Conn had predicted, two small, watery-looking shapes appeared ahead.

"That's it!" Conn yelled before Brad could even point to them. "Watch out for the beach!"

Before Brad could see the beach, he felt the boat's keel scrape on the rough bottom and leaping quickly over the side and into the water he hauled the boat up on the beach.

One of the lights they'd seen was in Captain Scott's tent and the boys ran for it as fast as they could.

Scott reacted immediately to their story. Before Brad had finished telling it, the tall Naval officer pulled on a raincoat and was moving toward the tent door.

"Let's go over to the ops room!" he snapped. "Surely Jordan will have it on the plot now."

CHAPTER 15

Mysterious Bush

WHEN BRAD and his friends reached the beach he immediately noticed an increase in the wind. Still coming from the west, it was strong enough now to have broken up the fog. The grey mist, still in patches, lay on the surface of the Bay but was thinning rapidly.

As they pushed Conn's dory into the deep water, the Nova Scotian raised his head in the air and sniffed.

"Feel that wind? It'll take some of the fog away but it's goin' to blow more and more."

"How soon, Conn?" the Captain queried.

"Maybe not tonight, sir, but tomorrow or tomorrow night for sure."

The increase in the wind had driven the chop on Mahone Bay up to something large enough to make the quick trip across to Grandall Point an uncomfortable one. In spite of the rising wind and the threat of rain, the sentry on the shore was alert enough to spot them before they'd hauled the boat up on the beach and clear of the waves.

Once again Captain Scott showed his identification card and explained who the boys were, though he didn't waste any time doing it. Together they moved through the trees and bushes as fast as they could, then dropped down in the elevator and rushed into the underground operations room.

"The boys were just out in the bay," snapped the Captain, when they joined Lieutenant Commander Jordan at his desk, "and they saw 'Le Grand'."

Without bothering to reply, Jordan switched on the radar set in front of his desk and fiddled with the knobs.

"Any unidentified contacts on the short range, MacDonald?" he called.

"No, sir," replied an officer from across the room. "The usual and the destroyer 'Cree' down from Halifax on exercises."

Jordan shook his head in bewilderment and again looked back at his own set.

Quickly the set clicked from contact to contact and at each of them a profile jumped into view. None of them looked like "Le Grand".

"I don't understand it!" cried Captain Scott.

Jordan shook his head slowly. "Neither do I, sir."

"Have you got a yacht on the screen?"

"If you mean the one that's been anchored off Oak Island, we have!"

Lieutenant Commander Jordan adjusted more dials and as Brad watched a profile of Dwight Davis' yacht "Esther" sprang into view.

"She's left the anchorage now, sir," Jordan said to Captain Scott, "and is heading out for the mouth of the Bay."

Looking as though it was etched on the screen, Brad could see the outline of the yacht. Her stub funnel and mast were in plain sight as was the cruiser stern. There was even a thickened portion of the echo on the flying bridge that Jordan told them was a man.

Watching the radar screen, Brad saw the range and bearing indicators click slowly to a halt and then stop. On the screen the yacht just sat in one position until another echo appeared. This one, much smaller, left "Esther" and moved off toward the northeast.

"That's a motor boat," explained Jordan, "and it looks as though it had two people aboard."

Then, abruptly, the contact stopped moving. Quickly Jordan reached down and adjusted the set's tuning. As far as Brad could see nothing happened on the screen, though portions of the contact seemed to get dimmer.

"What's the matter, Jordan?" snapped Captain Scott.

Lieutenant Commander Jordan was puzzled. "I don't know, sir. If there was another contact there I'd say that motor boat had come alongside another ship and had landed a couple of passengers, but that's impossible."

"Then, as far as you're concerned, there's no place for the passengers to have gone."

"That's right! Just a minute, sir!"

Jordan turned toward a man wearing earphones and sitting in front of what looked like a commercial tape recorder.

"Are you monitoring all the radio telephones?" he asked.

"Yes, sir!"

"Any transmissions from the yacht 'Esther'?"

"Not since early this morning. There was a talk then with some people in Halifax about a meeting at a party tonight."

Both Jordan and Captain Scott looked even more puzzled.

"That's all we can do, sir," Lieutenant Commander Jordan said. "There just isn't anything moving in our area that we can't account for."

Captain Scott was reluctant to give up but he could easily see there was nothing more to be done in the ops room. "We might as well go back to the camp, boys," he said slowly. "Maybe tomorrow we could go out and have another look at 'Esther'. Surely we could find an excuse."

On the way back to the surface, Brad was amazed at the construction of the underground operations room. When they left the elevator shaft he felt a slight rumble on the steel under his feet. Scott explained it as the pounding of the waves back on the beach.

"We're far enough underground," he said, "to make the vibrations felt. In fact the people who work down here all the time say they can tell what the state of the sea is like from the vibration of the steel."

"Is the whole place a steel shell?" Brad asked.

"Not completely. The steel just runs a few feet back from the elevator shaft. The rest is just brick heavy enough to hold the dirt walls up."

On the surface the wind was blowing even harder than it had before. When Brad saw the way the waves were crashing onto the beach he wondered how Conn would get the small boat ashore on Oak Island without giving them all a ducking.

He needn't have worried.

Conn turned the small boat into a position where the stern was directly facing the sea then he jammed the throttle full ahead. The boat leaped forward until, just at the right moment, he cut the throttle and hauled the motor over the stern. With a lift from the waves the boat grounded and leaping out into the ankle deep water Brad hauled it up on the beach high and dry.

"What now, sir?" he asked Captain Scott, when they got back to the tents.

"Nothing for tonight, as far as I can figure out. Tomorrow morning, though, I think we should make some excuse to get out to Davis' yacht. That gent has some explaining to do."

Brad worked on the notes for his feature stories for a while until it was nearly time for bed, then he stretched and suggested to Conn that they should go for a walk.

"I don't suppose the weather is all that good but I'm too excited to get to sleep right now."

"OKay, Brad," Conn agreed.

Leaving the camp the boys turned toward the west and walked through the stinging wind. The air was warm enough for them to be comfortable but Brad was happy he wasn't out in the Atlantic in a dory on such a night.

"What do you think happened to 'Le Grand'?" Brad asked when they'd walked through the trees and were going along the beach.

"I don't know, but no matter what that guy says in that fancy operations room with all those gadgets, we saw the ship. She's somewhere out in the Bay there."

Brad agreed but with all the best radar brains in the country using the best equipment available he couldn't understand why the ship wouldn't appear on the screens.

The boys had passed under the power lines leading from Oak Island to Grandall Point when, ahead of them, Brad saw some figures moving back and forth across the beach.

There were two boats on the beach and the shadowy figures were moving in a hurry from the boats to a dark spot just above the high water mark.

Grabbing Conn's arm Brad drew his friend back into the shelter of the trees.

Silently the boys watched for a while until Brad said. "Let's get a closer look."

As silently as ghosts they crept through the trees keeping the shadows between them and the beach. Crouching behind the oak tree boles, Brad and Conn watched the figures unloading several boxes and moving them toward a peculiar-looking bush. At the bush the men and the bundles they carried just disappeared into the earth.

"That's it!" Brad whispered.

"Whatta you mean?"

"When we were walking down here the other day I wondered what was peculiar about this stretch of beach. It was that bush growing there. It's the only one along here and it's a phony. They've got it fastened to some kind of a trap door and they're going down into a tunnel."

"Where to?" Conn asked, puzzled.

"I don't know! But it's not too far over to the naval ops room!"

"What'll we do?"

Brad could see there were too many men for he and Conn to tackle alone but somebody had to watch what was going on.

"I'll stay here on watch," he said. "You go back and get Captain Scott."

"OKay, Brad!"

With that, Conn ran back into the trees and Brad Forrest lay on the ground watching the men moving back and forth from the boats to the mysterious bush on the shore.

CHAPTER 16

Underground Fight

THE HOWLING of the wind across Mahone Bay covered any noise the men on the beach were making. Twice Brad saw the silhouette of a figure he was sure belonged to Dwight Davis directing the operations as the men rushed from the boats to the black spot on the beach.

"What is it, Brad?"

The boy jumped with fright when Captain Scott placed a hand on his shoulder. Alert as he was, the noise from the wind kept him from hearing Conn and the Naval officer as they crept up from behind.

"I'm sure Davis is out there," Brad explained. "They've been taking boxes of stuff down what looks like a tunnel, under that bush."

"How many are there?" snapped Scott.

"About six."

Captain Scott was silent for a moment. Brad

knew he was trying to make a decision on what to do.

"Things must be coming to a head for Davis, whatever he's up to," mused Scott. "What we have to find out is what he's doing."

"Let's have a look!" said Brad.

"Right! That's the only thing to do. We'll have to be careful."

Together the three friends crept across the beach toward the bush. There was no sign of a sentry and the roar of the storm would have covered their footsteps anyway.

"Let's put a hole in the boat so they can't get away," urged Brad.

Captain Scott shook his head. "Not now. If we can't stop them we might want to see where they go to from here."

The bush that seemed out of place on the beach covered an ingenious trap door. Brushing the sand away from its base, Brad tugged gently at the bush and it folded back.

In the dim light they could see a set of crude, steep stairs leading straight down into the earth.

"Holy Moses!" said Brad.

Captain Scott led the way down the stairs. The steps were carefully braced with bits of wood though each time they moved some earth trickled off to the next step.

Conn was the last man in the tunnel and he

Underground Fight 113

pulled the trap door tight behind him. Instantly the roar of the wind disappeared and all they could hear was the rumble of the sea underfoot and the sound of sharp voices ahead.

When the steps disappeared, the full width of the tunnel opened before them. It ran ahead in a fairly straight line widening out all the way with what looked like a small room piled high with boxes to one side just ahead.

Silently Scott moved forward waving the boys to follow him. They hadn't gone more than twenty five yards down the tunnel when ahead they could see a wider opening, bright with flashlights. Through the light several figures moved back and forth.

"That's far enough for now," the voice that was almost a snarl came from behind them.

Swinging around, the friends saw Jenkins, the man from the dig, stepping out of the little room with an automatic levelled at them.

"You didn't think Davis would try an operation like this without a guard, did you?" he said with an evil grin.

"Where is Davis?" Scott asked brusquely.

"You'll see, Captain. Just go straight ahead, slowly. I'll be right behind with my finger itching on the trigger of this gun."

"I never did trust you, Jenkins," snapped Scott.

"Too bad you didn't," snarled the crook. "If I'd

managed to slow you down at the dig enough, you'd have been off the island now and not giving us any trouble."

Jenkins waved the gun as though he meant it and with a set and stern look on his face Scott turned and strode down the tunnel with Brad and Conn following close behind.

"Look what I found!" Jenkins yelled, when the prisoners moved into the lighted area at the end of the tunnel.

Neither Brad nor his companions heard the crook. They were too amazed at what they saw spread out ahead of them.

Four of the men were scraping away the dirt from the wall directly ahead and a red brick wall was already showing in some places.

Peter Grey was one of the men working with a shovel!

Dwight Davis was plastering something that looked like a grey jelly to the wall and leading from an exploder box at his feet was a long line of wires.

"It's the wall of the ops room!" cried Brad.

Davis stepped away from the wall with a laugh. "Of course it is! But it won't be much of a wall for long."

"You'll never get away with it!" snapped Scott.

"Hah!" Davis' normally pleasant face was twisted in a sneer and his cold blue eyes were even more frosty than Brad remembered them. "All I

Underground Fight 115

need to do is get in there long enough to grab that profile indicator and then I'm on my way. The people I work for have the best radar equipment in the world but they haven't got a set like that. It's all we need."

While Davis was bragging about the way he was going to steal the radar indicator, Brad kept his eyes fixed on Peter Grey.

The ex-Naval officer had a small shovel in his hand and his face looked grim as he watched Scott and Davis talking. Brad didn't know whether Scott had noticed Grey, but with Grey on their side they might just be able to overpower the crooks before they set off the plastic explosive Davis had been putting on the walls.

As this thought flashed through his mind, Brad locked eyes with Grey.

Did Grey wink? Brad couldn't tell but he did notice the man's grip on his shovel tighten. Then Grey's eyes flicked from Brad to Jenkins and back to Brad again.

This time Brad saw Grey's wink distinctly.

When Grey leaped for Davis, Brad was ready to act.

Brad wondered if Captain Scott would be observant enough to see Grey was leaping for Davis but the boy needn't have worried.

As Grey leaped, both Conn and Scott moved.

Shifting his weight and swinging half around

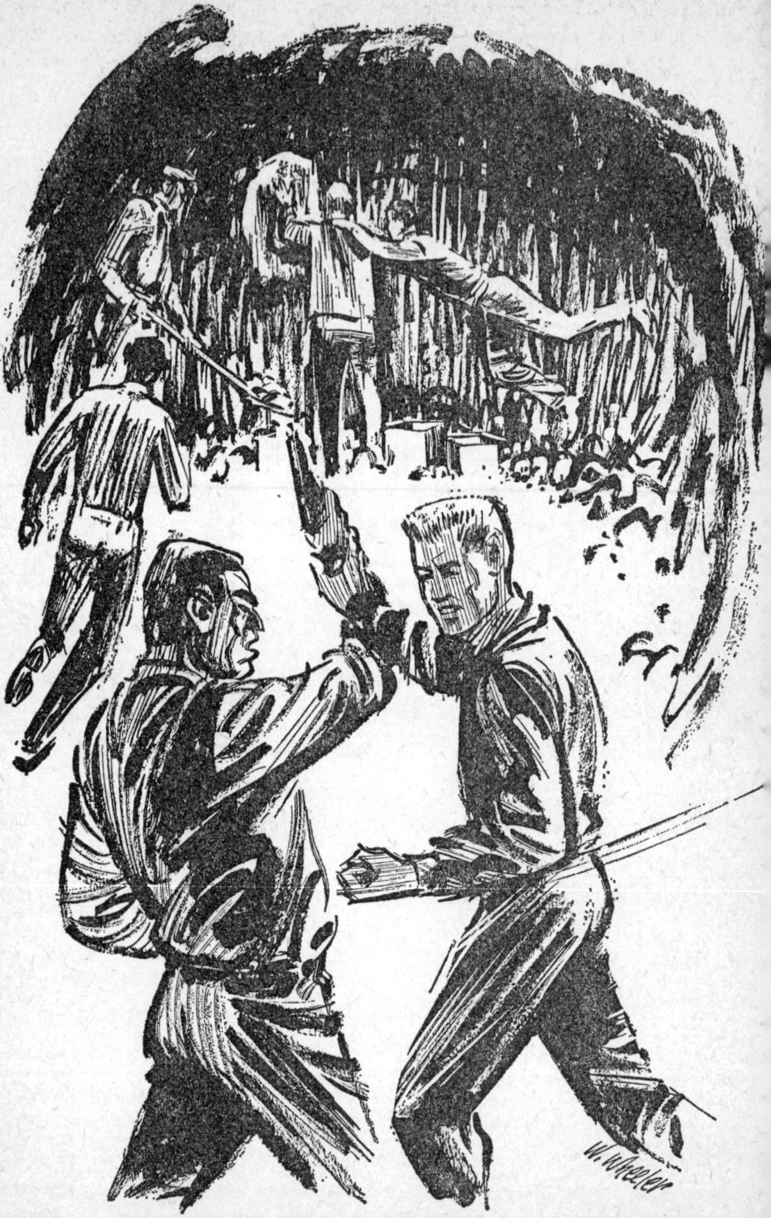
W. Wheeler

Underground Fight 117

on the ball of his left foot, Brad brushed Jenkins' automatic aside with his right hand and at the same time drove the toe of his left foot into Jenkins' knee. The movement of Brad's right arm was a continuous one and from the automatic it went straight up in the air and the palm of his hand crashed down in a perfectly placed judo chop on the back of the crook's neck.

Without his weight moving at all, Brad's fist drove into the pit of Jenkins' stomach.

"Whoosh!" The man lost his breath and Brad knew he was out of the fight.

The boy swung around ready to leap for one of the men at the wall.

Then he stopped!

Davis and Grey were wrestling on the dirt floor, Captain Scott had his man locked in a judo hold and Conn had the other.

Peter Grey was having trouble with Davis and Brad went to his assistance. It was two long jumps across the piles of dirt and rubble to reach the young Intelligence officer and on the second jump Brad tripped and fell.

His tough muscular body landed in a heap on Peter Grey's back and the unexpected weight threw Grey off Davis and rolled him on the floor.

Panting, Brad leaped to his feet. Grey was already there and the two were ready to jump for Davis.

They were too late!

As Brad watched, the crook scuttled through the tunnel entrance. Grey and Brad ran after him but they were just in time to see him disappear up the stairs.

When Brad looked up, the trap door cover slammed down. Pushing from below, Brad could only move the trap door a fraction of an inch. Tensing his muscles he pushed again but it was no use.

Davis had had time to move something on top of the door.

They were trapped underground and Davis was getting away.

CHAPTER 17

"Esther" Explodes

Leaping to the top step, Grey crowded in beside Brad.

"Together now!" he snapped, bracing his legs and jamming his hands against the door.

Using all their strength they both pushed up and against the door.

It was no use!

Brad felt the veins standing out on his head and he thought he could hear Grey's muscles creak but though the door raised just a trifle, when they relaxed, it fell back into place with a "clump".

"Get Captain Scott," snapped Grey. "I'll see if I can dig some of this sand away from the door edges."

"Leaving the Intelligence officer, Brad dashed back down the tunnel and panted out his information to the Captain.

"Watch these crooks!" Scott snapped to Conn. "If they move, shoot them! Common, Brad!"

At the top of the stairs Peter Grey had managed to dig away some of the sand holding the trap door in place but it wasn't enough for him to move it alone.

"Just a minute!" Brad cried. Then the boy ran back into the tunnel where Conn was holding the four crooks at bay.

A quick look around told him his deduction had been right and picking up two crowbars he sped back down to the trap door.

Brad used one bar and Captain Scott the other. Jamming the sharp point under the edge of the wooden door they threw all their weight on the bars while Grey pushed.

"One-two-three-heave!" cried Scott.

On the first heave the door moved and on the second it sprang open with a rumble as whatever Davis had jammed it with fell off.

"Peter!" ordered the Captain. "You get back down in that hole and help Conn herd those crooks out here on the beach! Brad you come with me! We'll alert the Navy Security guard and see if we can find Davis."

With that, Captain Scott sprang out of the tunnel and on to the beach with Brad close behind.

The wind was rising now and the loose sand

from the shore slammed into their faces when they got into the fresh air.

"It was that small boat," said Scott, pointing to the dinghy that had managed to roll off the trap door and over to its side.

Both the other boat and Davis had disappeared!

"Let's get our own boat!"

With Brad close behind, Captain Scott fought his way down the island against the force of the wind. They had trouble getting the small boat far enough out in the water to use the engine and they were both soaked. In the excitement, Brad didn't notice the cold water and the wind that cut right through him.

Captain Scott drove the boat at full speed around the tip of the Oak Island point and across the narrow hook of water to Grandall Point.

Pausing on the point just long enough to snap out orders to the sentry to round up the officer-of-the-guard, some men and two cutters, Scott bolted through the woods toward the entrance to the underground operations room.

After the howl of the driving wind outside, the silence inside struck Brad again. He was also impressed with the command Captain Scott had of the situation.

In spite of the near disbelief on Lieutenant Commander Jordan's face, he jumped into action when the Captain explained how they'd stopped a gang from blowing in a wall of the operations room.

"They're after that profile indicator," he finished. "But now we've got to get them before they get out of the Bay. What have you got on the screens?"

There was nothing but Davis' yacht "Esther" moving across the bay toward the entrance.

"He's in a hurry," said Lieutenant Commander Jordan.

For a second Captain Scott studied the screen. "He sure is," he said, "but we don't know where he's hurrying to. I'll get out there in one of the cutters."

"Can we stop him?" Brad asked, anxiously.

"Maybe we can!" put in the operations officer. "Don't forget we've got 'Cree' in the Bay doing exercises. She'll have steam up and be able to get under way in a couple of minutes."

Picking up a microphone, Lieutenant Commander Jordan pressed a couple of buttons and then was talking to the destroyer's Commanding Officer.

Giving "Cree" the bearing of the yacht and the speed showing on the radar screen, Jordan concluded his orders.

"Watch it, out there. We have reason to believe there's another ship moving around the Bay entrance that we want to stop from getting beyond the twelve mile limit. In the meantime, get on the

"Esther" Explodes

yacht's trail and pick up Captain Scott and his crew in a cutter. I'll keep you informed on this frequency where the cutter is until you have it on your own radar."

The officer on the destroyer understood the instructions perfectly. He had no questions, he just acknowledged the order in the traditional Navy fashion.

"On the way!" came the voice crackling through the loud speaker on the wall.

"So are we, Brad!" snapped Scott.

Outside, Captain Scott and Brad discovered the efficient officer-of-the-guard had taken in the situation at a glance. He'd organized a cutter to cross the narrow strip of water and pick up Conn, Peter Grey and their prisoners, all of them looking surly and dejected in the howling wind.

"Someday I'll get you!" Jenkins snarled at Brad.

"It won't be for a while," Captain Scott cut in, "you'll be our guests for a long time."

"Mebbe so! But you won't get Davis!"

"We'll see!"

"Let's get out there and see if we can find 'Esther'," he ordered.

The group went in two cutters. With a Navy coxswain in charge of their boat Brad, Conn, Captain Scott and Peter Grey headed out through the rising wind and sea of Mahone Bay. The other cutter, loaded with the Naval guard was close behind.

Brad had spent a lot of time in small boats but the ride across Mahone Bay was the wildest he'd ever had. The sturdy cutter pounded up and down in the heavy swell, its bow diving into the sea and then shrugging off the spray that came aboard.

"Head right out for the entrance," Captain Scott ordered.

For what seemed like hours, the small boat thumped and thudded through the sea. The spray driven into the air from the wave tops with the fog and darkness made visibility almost nil and they'd only gone a mile when they lost touch with the other boat.

"Shall I try and find it, sir?" called the coxswain over the shrieking of the wind.

"Never mind it now. Keep heading straight out and when we get there we'll go back and forth across the bay entrance."

"Be a bit like lookin' for a needle in a haystack," Conn murmured to Brad.

"I guess it will, but if the destroyer finds us we'll be OKay."

With nothing to go on but the few flashing lights from the buoys, the coxswain turned the cutter beam on the sea and began to make a sweep across the mouth of the bay. They were trying to do what

"Esther" Explodes

they could to seal up the area between Big Tancook Island and Heckman Island.

"Hope he doesn't try and slip out the other way," yelled Conn over the wind.

"All we can do is keep a good lookout," Brad replied.

Ahead of them were banks of fog in the darkness that time and time again looked like a ship. The coxswain altered the boat's course to head for each one but each changed into a cloud when they got closer to it.

Close to Big Tancook they were turning back for the mainland when ahead and off to port Brad saw a shape that looked more solid than the others they had been chasing.

"To port!" the boy yelled. "To port!"

As the coxswain pushed the boat's tiller over they all saw the fog clear away for an instant and there was "Esther" lying in the trough of the waves. The navigation lights were off but there were enough lights on the upper deck and shining through the portholes for them to be able to distinguish her.

At full throttle the small boat leaped across the waves toward the yacht.

"There's something wrong," called Captain Scott. "It looks to me as though she's been abandoned."

When they reached a point within a hundred

yards of the yacht, Brad saw something through the ports that looked like a brilliant glow of flame. For a second the light from inside the yacht made the water around it scarlet and then, with red flames shooting high in the air, the yacht blew up.

"W-h-u-m-p!" Almost slowly the sides moved out and the squat funnel leaped into the air. The mast started to totter and the whole bridge structure was enveloped in the white heat of the explosion.

"W-h-u-m-p! W-h-u-m-p!" There were two more explosions and in a cloud of flame and spray from the sea "Esther" disappeared from sight.

Overhead the clouds were brightened by the red of the flames and as the force of the explosion travelled, the waves bounced the cutter and its crew around.

Brad had never seen anything as horrible as the yacht's destruction. One minute it was floating and the next was a flaming hulk settling quickly under the sea.

"Golly!" Brad breathed.

The coxswain had stopped the boat and, fascinated, they all were staring at the wreck as it disappeared under the waves.

"What now, sir. . . ." Brad started to say as he turned around toward Captain Scott.

The boy didn't finish his sentence. As he turned

"Esther" Explodes

he could see beyond the Captain out into the bay where they had come from.

Looming through the darkness and heaving up and down in the sea, with a tremendous white wave in front of it, was a ship. It was heading right for them and in a second would cut them in two.

"Look!" Brad's scream was urgent enough to turn them all around to look in the direction of his pointing finger.

Horror-struck they stared at the eight thousand tons of certain death that was rushing down on them.

In the twinkling of an eye, the young sailor at the rudder recovered his wits. He jammed the throttle wide open and turned the cutter on a course that would take them away from the steel bow rushing down on them.

"We'll never make it!" thought Brad.

CHAPTER 18

Captured

THEY NEARLY did! But not quite!

The huge, hulking weight of "Le Grand" seemed to be leaping across the waves, as though shot from a gun, aimed perfectly at the small boat trying to get out of its path.

The boat's coxswain was smart enough not to try and run away from the ship. His course was across the ship's path. He knew just a couple of feet would make the difference between life and death for all of them.

"Coxswain..." Captain Scott started to scream out some orders and then stopped, realizing the young sailor was doing all he could.

Half standing in the cutter and gripping a gunwhale with one hand and a thwart with the other Brad watched the ship rushing down at them. Her range was just enough for him to see over the bows and to the superstructure amidships.

Captured

Like most of the older merchant ships, "Le Grand" was built with three separate structures above the flat surface of the deck. Three island ships they were called.

Over the midships' structure and right on top of the wheelhouse and chartroom was monkey's island, a spot with a compass and wheel that could be used for directing the ship coming into harbour.

On monkey's island Brad could see two figures. One directing the ship and one steering it.

The boy was sure one of the figures was Dwight Davis, but before he could give it any attention the flare of the ship's bow got in the way.

As the two people on monkey's island disappeared, Brad felt the cutter bounce in another direction as the water pushed ahead of the ship reached the small boat. The cutter was tossed nearly on its port side and Brad saw the coxswain reach into the control box and make some final, desperate adjustments.

Brad could feel the small boat surge ahead after the last throttle adjustment and then "Le Grand's" bow was past them and they were enveloped by the mountain of water she was displacing.

So close was the ship to the boat that as the enormous hulk raced past them, Brad reached out and tried to push them away from the rusty side.

They bumped twice and then three times down the ship's side. Each crash of the steel plates of the ship against the cutter tore the wood and threw the boat into the confused water nearby.

When they were sucked toward the propellers Brad knew that all was lost.

"Get over the side!" yelled Captain Scott, his voice cracking as he strained it against the wind.

In instant obedience to the orders, the coxswain and Peter Grey dove from the boat into the dark, rough waters of Mahone Bay. Brad saw Captain Scott leaping just ahead of him but for the moment Conn Casey was lost from his sight.

In the water the boy looked over his shoulder just long enough to see the 27-foot navy cutter tumble in the air, stern high. Even over the roaring of the wind and the noise from the ship's engines he heard the crash as the boat turned turtle and landed bottom side up.

Brad and his friends in the water kept together as they watched the huge hull of "Le Grand" stop, with a foaming under the stern and then turn slowly toward them.

"They're coming back for us!" Brad yelled.

"Watch it!" Peter Grey called through the wind's roar. "They might be coming back to finish the job."

When the freighter turned she didn't head for them at full speed as the Naval officer had said but sidled up through the waves with a scramble net and two rope ladders hanging over the side.

Captured

Brad felt wet and miserable when he made his way over "Le Grand's" rusty iron railing and dropped down on the deck. Surrounding them was as tough and mean looking a group of men as he'd seen for some time. Two of the faces he recognized from the brief glimpse he'd had of them in the house in Halifax.

Where was Conn?

Brad's Nova Scotian friend had disappeared. At least he wasn't among the group looking miserable and staring at a gloating Dwight Davis who was running down the iron deck toward them.

"Where's...?"

Brad was going to ask if the others had seen Conn but then he thought better of it. If the boy had gotten away there was no sense setting Davis and his vicious crew after him.

"Take them up to my cabin!" Davis ordered. "Lock them in while I get the ship back on course."

Davis' cabin was a big one just under the ship's centre superstructure. From the thumping of feet overhead Brad could tell it was just beneath the wheelhouse.

Miserably the four friends flopped down on the settees and chairs in the cabin. Brad knew there would be nothing but trouble ahead for them and unless the destroyer "Cree" managed to stop "Le Grand" they could never get out of *this* spot.

When Davis arrived he just slammed and locked

the door behind him while he looked around. Then he strode over to where Peter Grey was lying on the deck and kicked the young officer hard in the ribs.

"That's for fooling us!" the man snarled.

"You won't get away with this!" Captain Scott cried. "There's a destroyer on the way out here right now."

"Maybe I won't!" snapped Davis, swinging around to face the Captain. "I didn't get my job done either but you won't be here when the destroyer arrives."

"What was your so-called job anyway?" asked Brad.

"I was after that profile indicator in the underground ops room you think is such a secret. The people I work for have every bit as much radar equipment as you have but they haven't got that. They would have paid me anything for it."

"What's the equipment you have on board here?" asked Grey, shrewdly.

"You mean the gear that makes us invisible to a radar set? Your country will never find out. But considering you'll just be with us a few more minutes I'll give you some idea."

"What do you mean invisible?"

"Just that. Invisible to radar. The gear in the hold and the gear in the scuppers is just a refinement of the wartime Degaussing gear that was used to counter the effect of magnetic mines.

Captured

"This equipment provides a cushion as sort of an absorbing envelope that sucks in the radar transmission from your sets and sends nothing back. We've had this for years and your people have been too stupid to know it."

"How long have you been working at that tunnel from Oak Island to the ops room?" asked Captain Scott.

"All summer. I brought the men up here with me in "Esther" and even only working at night we would have made it perfectly if this kid hadn't managed to stumble on that phony bush on the beach.

"That's why I planted Jenkins on your work gang. He was supposed to make it so difficult for you you'd give up."

Davis' mouth clamped shut tight and his frosty eyes gleamed when he went on. "Like so many other things we just had bad luck."

"Was it one of your people that hit me on the head and tossed me in the bay?" Brad asked.

"That was another warning to you. You'll wish you'd taken it before this night is through."

"How did . . .?" Before Brad could finish his question, Davis waved his arm for silence.

"That's enough talk. If I'm going to put you ashore I've got to make some arrangements."

"Ashore!" cried Scott. "What do you mean?"

Davis paused at the door. "Just what I say! On the ground—but twenty fathoms down!"

Before the friends could take in what he meant, the crook slammed the door behind him and they could hear the key turn in the lock.

CHAPTER 19

Away Boarders!

"What . . . ah . . . what did he mean, sir?" the coxswain's voice trembled when Davis had left for the bridge.

"It's not good!" snapped the officer. "But don't worry! 'Cree' is somewhere out here in the bay looking for us and they won't get away with it."

Brad knew exactly what Dwight Davis had been talking about and his usual bright, cheerful outlook disappeared when he thought about being tossed over the side in this storm.

"Every minute we wait here is all the better for us," Peter Grey put in cheerfully. "I think Davis is probably crazy enough that he doesn't really believe 'Cree' is on the hunt for him. Though with all the modern radar equipment they have they must be able to keep track of everything that's moving in the bay."

"Wonder what we can do to stall him?" Brad asked, from his position on the floor.

"Anything would help," said Scott. "Anything!"

They didn't have long to wait for Davis to reappear. Now the crook was accompanied by two other sailors and a sentry carrying a machine gun. Davis called the sentry Harris.

"On your feet!" he snapped.

When nobody moved, he motioned the two men forward. "OKay! Just stay there and be dragged out on deck."

"Just a minute, Mr. Davis," said Brad. "I want to talk to you."

"What do *you* want?"

"I don't see what I've got to do with this," said Brad in a wheedling tone. The expression on the boy's face had changed to one of submission and his eyes had a pleading, frightened look in them. "I only came down here to write a couple of stories. I didn't have anything to do with this. I was only an innocent bystander."

"So what!" Davis snapped.

"You traitor!" yelled Captain Scott. "What are you trying to say?"

"I can't help it!" Brad pleaded. "I don't want to be tossed overboard, even if the rest of you don't care."

Away Boarders! 137

Then the boy turned to the crook. "Maybe we can make some kind of a deal, sir."

"A deal! What kind of a deal?"

"I don't really know, but maybe I could give you some help in getting the gear you want from the operations room."

"Stop!" screamed Grey. With that the Naval officer leaped across the room toward the boy, his fists raised.

Before he made it, one of the guards stepped forward and jammed the muzzle of his machine gun into Grey's stomach.

"That's enough!" snapped Davis. "You must think I'm stupid to be fooled by that act!"

Brad opened his mouth to start to speak again when Davis waved his hand for silence and motioned for the guards to herd them out of the cabin.

"Nice try, Brad," said Captain Scott warmly. "That was a brave thing to do."

Brad didn't say anything. It hadn't been much of a bluff but it had been something to delay the crook even for a few minutes.

From "Le Grand's" amidships superstructure Brad, Captain Scott, Grey and the young sailor were pushed out to the ship's after deck and into the teeth of the howling gale.

"Over to port," yelled Davis. "Watch 'em, Harris!"

Pushed against their will toward the port rail, the group were held in a tight circle by the menacing guns of the guards. Before they could move, two of the guards wrapped several lengths of chain around their legs and tied them with rope.

"That'll do it," said Davis. "It's not much but it should be enough to take them down."

"It's murder!" cried the coxswain.

"You'll never get away with this!" Captain Scott cried. "'Cree' will catch up with you before you get out of the Bay."

"Over the side with them," ordered Davis to the men standing beside him grinning.

Brad knew it was too late to struggle on the ship's deck. All they could do was get over the side without being shot and see if they could get free of the chains before they were dragged to the bottom.

They went over in a group. Brad, Captain Scott and Peter Grey were tight lipped but as Brad tumbled over the rail, with the heavy chains tearing into his leg, he could see the panic on the young sailor's face.

"... together!" Captain Scott had yelled something as they fell through the air but the noise of the wind and the pounding of the ship's engines drowned out all but the last word.

Brad ducked his head as they fell through the air and when the ice-cold water, churned into huge

Away Boarders!

waves by the wind, closed over him, he was tearing at the strands of rope holding the chain to his leg.

The four surfaced in a group. Ahead of them Brad could see the rusty steel side of "Le Grand" moving past them at what seemed like a tremendous speed.

From the way the Captain and Grey were working at the chains on their legs, Brad knew they would be fighting to the last for their lives.

But the coxswain was too young to understand you never give up and from the way he thrashed around in the water, Brad could tell he was panic-stricken.

One more tug and the chains holding Brad Forrest's legs together dropped off. Catching just a glimpse of "Le Grand" disappearing to their left through a fog bank and the darkness, the boy turned his attention to saving the sailor.

"Easy!" Brad shouted. The height of the waves breaking over their heads and the roar of the storm pulled the words out of his mouth and tossed them away in the wind.

The sailor flung his arms up in the air and when Brad reached his side he knew the youngster would sink in a moment. To get his attention, Brad slapped him hard on the side of the head and then beating off the attempt to grab his neck, Brad ducked under the water and began to struggle with the chain on the young man's legs.

Together they dropped beneath the surface!

When the water closed over his head, Brad was immediately conscious of the fact because the noise of both wind and sea disappeared abruptly. Trying to hold the boy's legs still he yanked at first one strand of rope and then another. Feeling the one on the right leg give, Brad reached for the sailor's left leg, at the same time ducking out from under the hands that were clutching for him.

Brad's lungs were nearly bursting! He knew he could hold out no longer without air and when the sailor's body suddenly went limp it meant the young man he was trying to rescue had sucked in enough water to lose consciousness.

Brad wouldn't let him go!

Swinging around in the cold, silent depths of the water he grabbed the sailor's shirt front and then drove for the surface. With the body hanging limp from his arms and the heavy chain dangling from one leg it was nearly an impossible job.

Using the hardest scissor kick he had ever used and pushing at the water with his free hand Brad struggled toward the night air of Mahone Bay. There was a burning sensation in his lungs now and just as his head started to twirl, in the first sign of losing consciousness, he broke into the air.

Sucking in oxygen, Brad didn't forget the boy he was trying to save and he shifted his grip from the sailor's shirt to his chin. In spite of the weight

Away Boarders!

dragging the young man down, Brad got his face into the air.

As he wondered how he was going to keep the sailor above the surface and get the chain free, Brad felt two arms slip under his shoulders and before he could struggle, lift him out of the water.

Panting and spitting out mouthfuls of the sea Brad flopped over the thwart of a boat that was half filled with water. Raising his head he could see Captain Scott and Peter Grey dragging the sailor, with the chain still fast to his leg, from the sea.

Beyond the Captain was Conn Casey!

Conn! Where had he come from?

As Brad lay over the thwart watching the young sailor being hauled from the water he saw Conn bailing as fast as he could, trying to give the boat enough freeboard so she wouldn't sink.

Then he knew what'd happened! Conn must have stayed with the cutter when it tumbled over and, using all his skill, righted the boat and gotten out enough water so it would be light enough to move.

"Good old Conn!" Brad thought.

Still coughing, Brad lurched to his feet to move aft and give Conn what help he could. Still weak from his experience in the water he stumbled as he tried to stand up and catching hold of a gunwale for balance he looked across the water toward the shore.

"A ship!" he croaked. He coughed out another mouthful of water and then called, louder this time.

"A ship! It's a destroyer!"

It was "Cree"! In just a few moments the swift, sleek naval vessel pulled alongside them and down the scramble nets came a dozen sailors who hauled them from the waterlogged cutter and up to the safe, dry deck.

"Now what?" thought Brad. They were safe but Davis and "Le Grand" were still getting away.

As the boy pulled himself to his feet he could feel the rumble of the destroyer's screws as she got under way again. Still coughing, he ran along the deck behind Captain Scott as the tall Naval officer headed for the bridge.

"Do you know where 'Le Grand' is?" Captain Scott was asking the "Cree" Commanding Officer, when Brad joined him.

The ship's Captain was just shaking his head with a puzzled look on his face. "We've investigated every contact in the Bay that's large enough to be a merchant ship and none of them answer the description you gave Lieutenant Commander Jordan."

"Let's have a look! Common, Brad!"

With Peter Grey and Conn close behind, the group rushed into the destroyer's Combat Information Centre. Brad no more than glanced around the

Away Boarders! 143

room, that was a maze of radar screens, plotting table and telephones, when Captain Scott spoke up.

"Isn't there *anything* suspicious on the screens?"

"There's just this mushy spot, sir," said the sailor operating the close range set. "We've had it all night. It's not like any contact I ever saw."

"That'll be it!" snapped Scott. "I'll explain later. In the meantime cut that ship off so he can't get out of the Bay."

The Commanding Officer of the ship showed his training when he asked no questions. He just picked up a microphone and Brad heard his voice boom through the CIC.

"Port twenty! Come to course 196. One seven five revolutions."

Brad felt the destroyer shudder as her speed increased and he grabbed for support as she heeled slightly when the sea hit her beam.

"We'll be alongside her in about ten minutes, Captain Scott. What then?"

"We'll have to stop her."

The ship's Commanding Officer looked puzzled. "How, sir? Shall I clear away the guns?"

"No! We're too close to shore. We'll use a boarding party."

CHAPTER 20

Grounded

"Cree's" captain didn't blink when Scott gave his orders. Brad knew boarding parties hadn't been used in the Navy for years but "Cree" was ready.

"Call out the boarding party," the Commanding Officer said to his second-in-command who had appeared, as if by magic, at his shoulder. "We'll use both boats. Also, have the guns warmed through and trained athwartships."

"Aye, aye, sir!"

Brad was amazed at the activity the orders started. On all sides men were running back and forth and from the loud hailing system orders were blared out all over the ship.

For less than ten minutes, Brad and his friends kept their eyes glued to the radar screen watching the semi-circular pip that was "Cree" close on the dull, mushy spot they were hoping was "Le Grand".

"Let's go on deck, sir," said "Cree's" Captain.

"We should be able to get her in the searchlight now."

On deck the storm was raging as hard as ever. The destroyer was making a tight turn to the right and in turning she dropped into the trough of the seas that were pounding into Mahone Bay from the southeast. The sturdy little ship leaped from wave crest to trough and burying her nose into the sea shook only slightly as she rose for another wave.

All around them was darkness with the fog blown into patches by the wind. On deck two of the ship's boats had been turned out and standing, waiting to board were a large group of men.

"Do you wish to go, sir?" Captain Scott was asked.

"I sure do!" the Captain replied.

"We all do!" cried Brad. "I was in at the start of this and I don't want to be left behind now."

"OKay! Into the first boat. I'll get up on the bridge and take over now."

With Captain Scott, Conn and Peter Grey, Brad climbed into the forward cutter as it was swung out over the ship's side.

As they watched, "Cree" made another sharp turn to starboard and then, from overhead, a searchlight leaped out into the darkness. For a second it played back and forth across the sea and then, guided by the radar bearing being fed into it, fixed itself on the rolling rusty-looking hulk of "Le Grand".

Brad jumped when from "Cree's" bridge a tremendously loud voice bellowed into the night.

"'Le Grand'! Heave to! We are boarding you!"

Nothing happened on "Le Grand's" upper deck for a second and then men started to run back and forth, coming from alleyways and open doors. Most of them ran for the bridge and leaped into the wheelhouse with the last man slamming the door behind him.

But the ship didn't stop!

She ploughed straight ahead and once again from "Cree's" Captain came the warning shout. Then Brad saw the disturbance in the water at "Le Grand's" stern disappear, momentarily.

"Her engines have stopped," yelled Captain Scott, pointing.

They had and then with a violent thumping they could hear over the roar of the wind the propellers started in reverse. With that, "Cree" shuddered to a halt, just a hundred yards from "Le Grand" and down went the boats.

The destroyer was still moving when the cutter's coxswain yelled an order, pulled a handle and they crashed down into the water. A line forward was still attached to the destroyer and for a second they

Grounded 147

bounced from wave to wave as they were pulled along.

Without an order, the boat's bowman cast the rope loose as the engine started and they were on the way.

Brad was amazed at how skilfully it was done.

It was a short, but rough, trip across to "Le Grand" and on the way Brad and his friends watched, fascinated at the activity around the ship's bridge.

Half the distance was gone when suddenly the wheelhouse door was flung open and Davis and Harris leaped out to the flying bridge. With a machine gun clutched in his arms the crook forced a group of men back into the wheelhouse while Davis slammed the door and locked it from the outside.

"I'll bet the men made Davis stop the ship!" Captain Scott yelled into Brad's ear. "If he heads for the monkey's island now she'll start up again for sure."

That's exactly what happened!

In the glare of the searchlight, both Harris and Davis were terrifying figures. Harris was waving the gun around like a crazy man and Davis, with the wind tearing at his hair and clothes, headed straight for the exposed wheel and engine room controls.

That was all Brad saw then. The two cutters from "Cree" were alongside and when they threw the grappling hooks up to the rail they heard the ship's engines start again.

Captain Scott was first up "Le Grand's" side and Brad was close behind. When he jumped down on the iron deck the boy reached down and hauled Conn up after him.

"Take some men and get to the engine room!" the Captain ordered one of "Cree's" officers. "The rest of you get up to the wheelhouse and let those men out."

With the upper-deck brightly lit by "Cree's" searchlight they sped away on their jobs.

"We'll go after Davis and Harris," said Captain Scott.

As they climbed the ladder to the boat-deck, Brad felt the ship list to one side as Davis turned her hard to starboard. When they reached the top of the ladder Brad suddenly saw a spurt of small flame coming from the monkey's island and through the wind heard the rattle of machine gun fire.

"Back!" yelled Captain Scott. "They're not fooling!"

Together the four friends crouched back on the steel ladder not daring to expose their heads. In the glare of the light that made it bright as day they could never move across to the wheelhouse ladder without being cut to pieces by the gun.

"He'll have to douse that light!" Brad muttered.

Almost as though the "Cree's" Captain could read his mind the voice from the ship came leaping across the waves.

"I can see both you and the bridge. If you want me to adjust the light wave your arms."

Captain Scott waved his arms in the air and the light went out. After the glare of the light the darkness was complete.

"That'll help Harris just as much as us," Brad thought.

The man on "Cree's" searchlight had thought the same thing for as they watched the light came on again this time with the beam narrowed until it rested on monkey's island, blinding the crooks there.

The boat deck was in total darkness!

"Common!" snapped Captain Scott. Speeding across the wooden deck they could hear the rattle of the machine gun again as Harris tried to put out the light.

Crouching at the bottom of the only ladder leading to monkey's island, Captain Scott gave them their orders.

"Peter and I'll go up the ladder," he said. "Brad you and Conn go forward around the other side and climb up over the bridge dodger. When you hear us shout jump for the gun. Don't worry about Davis right now."

With that Conn nudged Brad in the ribs and together they moved to "Le Grand's" starboard side and started across the bridge. Ahead of them the steel windscreen loomed and just above was monkey's island, bright in the glare of the searchlight.

As Brad and Conn raised themselves to leap for the top of the windscreen, Conn grabbed his friend's arm and pulled him back to the bridge.

"Holy Moses!" he said. "He's goin' to put her on Whaleback Rock!"

"What do you mean?" Brad's voice was tight with urgency.

"Look!" Conn pointed ahead.

Just ahead and to port could be seen the rapid flashing of a red light. "That rock sticks up even in high water," cried Conn. "He's going to sink her."

"Cree's" Captain must have seen this just at the same moment. Through the blackness and over the wind's roar the voice of the bullhorn screamed.

"Whaleback Rock just ahead. He's trying to hole her!"

Though a thousand possibilities flashed through his mind there was nothing Brad could do at that moment. With the engines pounding full ahead and with Davis standing in the bright light screaming at the wind the ship ran full into the rock with a force that threw Brad and Conn off their feet.

CHAPTER 21

Davis Captured

BRAD COULDN'T believe it for a second.

Why should Davis run the ship aground and try to kill himself and them all?

The boy knew there was no time for such thoughts as this as he watched "Le Grand's" bows crumple over the rock that, at high tide, was barely sticking out through the water.

The bow kept moving over the rock and though the wind was howling and Davis' screams could be heard from overhead, the boy could hear the tearing of the steel plates as the boat worked its way up on the rock, driven by the powerful engines down below.

With the huge confused waves breaking over the bows, Brad and Conn gripped the bridge rail, hard, as they watched the ship come to a full stop with her bows pointing up in the air.

She was pushed up on the rocks well beyond

the hold on the forward deck and when he looked astern Brad saw the ship's after part sag as the full weight dragged it down into the deep water.

"Her back'll break!" Conn shouted against the wind. "She'll come apart any minute."

As his Nova Scotian friend yelled, Brad felt the huge ship sag again and there was another creaking of the tortured metal as the ship broke in half behind them.

The harsh glare of "Cree's" light showed Brad everything there was to see above the water and watching he saw the whole stern of the ship, aft of the bridge, part from the forward section and drop slowly into the deep water.

Now, two searchlights had burst into the blackness of the night from "Cree". One remained fixed on the bridge while the other played on the sinking stern and the men who were leaving the engine room and leaping into the rough waters of the bay.

"What about Davis and Harris?" shouted Brad. "They must be trying to kill themselves."

"Let's find out!"

When he yelled, against the wind, Conn wriggled up on the bridge rail and leaped for the monkey's island rail overhead. Brad was close behind.

When the boys jumped to the flat surface of monkey's island they were in the direct beam of "Cree's" light.

Davis Captured

Harris had fallen forward with the force of the impact when the ship ran aground and though his head had struck the compass binnacle he wasn't knocked right out. With the machine gun still grasped in his arms he was just trying to get to his feet when the boys rushed across the deck toward him.

As the machine gun came up to a firing position, Conn launched himself toward the crook in a flying leap.

"Get Davis!" he screamed.

Brad swung round in a tight circle just in time to see Dwight Davis leaping toward him.

The boy swerved just a bit to the left and as the man's charge moved past him the boy threw a terrific punch at the crook's right ear.

Brad missed!

It wasn't by much but just enough to throw him off balance and carry him down to the deck in a heap. The boy rolled over and came to his feet again, ready for the next charge or ready to charge himself.

Just ahead he saw Conn had subdued Harris to the point where the Nova Scotian was wrestling the crook's machine gun from his arms.

Then, on the other side of the bridge, he saw Davis disappear over the rail.

If he was going to catch Davis there was no time to worry about Conn not being able to take care of his man. Vaulting over the figures wrestling on the deck, Brad made for the disappearing crook.

When he jumped he was in the air for just a second but it was enough for him to feel the force of the wind move his body to one side.

Davis didn't bother with the vertical ladder leading from monkey's island to the bridge, he jumped, and when Brad got to the edge the crook was climbing the bridge rail ready to throw himself into the sea.

The rain and wind had soaked the crook so his clothes clung to his body like a bathing suit. His thick hair was blowing in the wind and just before he leaped into the fierce sea he looked back over his shoulder.

"You'll never get me alive!" he screamed.

Then he leaped! But Brad Forrest was right behind him.

The boy got to the bridge rail just as Davis was hitting the water and when he jumped he had just a glimpse of Captain Scott and Peter Grey running across the bridge toward him.

Brad hit the water feet first exactly in the spot where Davis had disappeared. The jump was high enough that the shock ran through his legs and into his back. He felt partly stunned when he surfaced but he wasn't so confused that he forgot Davis.

The crook had come to the surface just ahead of him but he was limp.

Davis Captured

It flashed through Brad's mind the jar of impact on the water had been enough to knock Davis out. He could drown in a moment and then all of Brad's effort would have been wasted.

The boy reached for the unconscious crook as the enormous waves from Whaleback Rock and the suction that followed them grabbed both Brad and Davis, sucking them toward certain death on the razor-sharp points of the reef.

Brad knew afterwards there must have been shouts at this point, but all he saw, at the moment, was the white circle of the life ring as it flew through the air and splashed on the disturbed water's surface.

With one hand Brad got a firm grip on the life ring and with the other reached for the crook.

The shirt Davis was wearing nearly tore out of his hands but the boy managed to pull the crook back from the force of the suction and into the safety of the floating ring held into position by the line coming from the boat beyond the torn stern of the broken freighter.

Brad shifted his grip from Davis' shirt to a cross-chest carry and still hanging tight to the ring it was just a matter of moments before he was dragged to safety.

The boy had nearly passed out himself but he remembered being in one of "Cree's" boats and climbing up the destroyer's side while Captain Scott, Conn and Peter Grey congratulated him on saving the crook's life.

He began to feel like himself an hour later in "Cree's" wardroom when he was wrapped in thick navy blankets and drinking hot chocolate. The destroyer was pounding into the storm heading for Chester.

"What do you think Davis was trying to do?" Brad asked the Naval officer.

"He was trying to keep the radar secrets on 'Le Grand' away from us. And he might have yet!"

"What do you mean?"

"All the gear, that means anything, in 'Le Grand', is kept in the part that sunk. There must be thirty fathoms of water where the ship's stern has gone down and all we can hope is that navy divers manage to get some of that stuff off."

"Gee!" said Brad. "Does that mean we failed?"

"Cheer up! We didn't fail at all. I was only trying to keep Davis from getting into the ops room so anything we can get from 'Le Grand' will be a bonus."

For a while Brad just relaxed in the comfort of the thick blankets and drank his hot chocolate. Then suddenly he remembered he'd been sent down to Halifax to get a story about the Oak Island treasure.

"What about the treasure?" he asked. "Are you going to keep on digging for it?"

"You're darn right! We haven't given it much time in the last week but now we have Davis and his gang safely tucked away we can get back to digging."

"Can I write a story about all this?" the boy asked.

Captain Scott was silent for a moment. "Not with all the details you can't, Brad. I'm sorry, security regulations would never permit it. You can write something about Peter Grey being underground to help the government. That'll be a real scoop for you."

"Thanks!" cried the boy. "Even that's more than I expected."

"I'll never forget you for the help you've given me," said Captain Scott.

Brad just smiled.

"Look!" hooted Conn Casey. "He's blushing!"

"Do you head back for Montreal after you write some stories about the treasure?" asked Peter Grey.

"Yeh! And then back to school."

"You'll have to come down here for the whole summer next year!" cried Conn. "I'll really show you the coast."

"Next summer I'm going to work in our London office," said the boy.

He might have gone to Halifax if he'd known

what would be waiting for him in **"BRAD FOR-REST'S LONDON ADVENTURE"**.

"London won't be anything like Nova Scotia!" cried Conn.

"No," Brad laughed. "I don't think so!"